A Beth-Hill Novel:
Wild Hunt Series, Book 6:
Family Matters

By Jennifer St. Clair

Writers Exchange E-Publishing

http://www.writers-exchange.com

Chapter 1

The explosion--or crash, because she heard glass breaking amid the noise of destruction--pulled Celeste away from the loom and to the front windows of her little cottage. She'd rented it with full knowledge that the property butted up against a vampire Household, but her landlord--a human wizard named Thomas Crone--had told her the Walkers were quiet neighbors who usually kept to themselves.

She hadn't, however, quite gathered up the courage to introduce herself to her new neighbors. Nefir would have been fascinated, of course, but he did not know where she lived--or he hadn't found her yet, at least, *this* time-- and she'd left Faerie to escape from both court drama *and* the king.

There was a dark, car-shaped blot in the ditch past the trees at the end of her driveway. The driver had swerved--or been forced off the road, she thought, because there was another car on the road, lights off, a taller SUV, and another one behind it. And flashlights, now, piercing the darkness but not the wards; she was safe behind them, at least. If these were vampire hunters, they wouldn't come back this far.

She thought she recognized the car in the ditch as an older model with tinted windows--one from the Walker compound. The interior light came on once as one of the men--she was certain now that they were Hunters, but she had no way to warn her neighbors, if they didn't already know--pulled open the door, and she heard the sound of a muffled shot. And then the smell of something burning, hanging heavy in the air.

The sky had subtly lightened as she watched, and she almost missed the slight figure who darted between the trees at the end of the driveway and vanished into shadow. From its furtive movements, Celeste doubted it belonged to the two cars on the road. But if there was someone missing from the crash, surely the Hunters would be searching the trees and the rest of the ditch? Their search had been fairly circumspect, an afterthought only.

The spark of a flame caught her eye. The men had set the wreck on fire. The figure in the shadows lurched forward, then fell back, farther into darkness now, even as the sky turned from black to grey.

From the end of the driveway, and even halfway down the driveway, the cottage wasn't visible at all, although Celeste's view of the road was unhindered. She opened the front door and stepped onto the porch as the men made one last desultory sweep of the ditch, then climbed back into their cars and sped away.

For a moment, the only sound was the crackle of flames.

Celeste waited for a moment to make sure they wouldn't return, then stepped off the porch and walked into the trees. She found the survivor lying at the foot of one of the young oaks, bleeding profusely from what looked to be bullet wounds, his eyes closed, seemingly unconscious. He couldn't have been more than fourteen, at best, with brown hair and a thin face now spotted with blood.

She had no idea if he were vampire or human, but she couldn't leave him lying there, regardless. So she brought an old rag rug from inside the house, rolled him onto it, and dragged him around the back where there weren't any steps.

In the light of the kitchen, he looked much worse; the thinness more pronounced, but the blood wasn't pumping from the wound over his heart anymore, and it actually looked like it was trying to close.

So a vampire, then. Cautiously, Celeste knelt beside him and set her meager Healing talent to work to find the bullets.

And they *were* bullets; six of them; three had gone through, but she dug out the others before the wounds could fully close. She found a cell phone in his pocket, but no identification, and a quick scan of the stored numbers did not help, although the entries marked "Mom" and "Dad" gave her pause. Should she call them? What if Mom and Dad had been in the car with their son and the Hunters had taken their cell phones to see who called?

Sirens approached now; a fire truck and an ambulance, and behind them, a police car. Celeste was vaguely surprised to find out it was dawn.

"They were--already dead," the vampire whispered, as if the ambulance siren had made her question the possibility of survivors. "That's why I--didn't go back."

Celeste glanced down at him. "Who were they?" she asked gently.

The vampire closed his eyes. "My parents. Both human." He opened his eyes again. They glittered with tears. "You're--" His eyes widened.

"An elf, yes," Celeste said. "Your neighbor, actually. I hadn't quite gotten up the courage to introduce myself quite yet."

His eyes abruptly cleared. "The weaver? Oh. Rebecca intended to ask you for lessons, if you--I didn't know you were an elf." He tried to smile, but it quivered at the edges and threatened to crumble. "I've never actually met an elf before."

"And I've never actually met a vampire before," Celeste said. "My name is Celeste."

"Ethan Walker," the vampire said, but she'd already guessed that, in truth, because it was a bit of a local legend that the heads of the Walker Household were humans, and that they had a vampire son.

The sun shone bright now, outside. The ambulance had driven away, its services unneeded. Celeste hadn't noticed if they'd taken the bodies from the car, or left them there for the police to handle. The police car remained with the fire truck, and one other car--another familiar Walker car--had arrived. The driver had emerged to speak to the policeman. There were others in the car with him, but they stayed in their seats.

"They'll be looking for me," Ethan whispered.

"You're stuck here until dusk, I'm afraid," Celeste said. I don't have a garage or any way to shelter you from the sunlight. And I doubt you can walk anyway; you've lost too much blood. You're lucky they weren't using silver bullets."

"I'd already be dead," Ethan said, and tried to force his arms to bear his weight. Celeste helped him sit up, but he didn't try to stand. "If you don't mind, could you let them know I'm alive? If there are any of my family here yet?"

Celeste described the man and the girl she could see in the passenger seat. "My sister Elizabeth," Ethan whispered. "Human. Andrew. Also human." His eyes slipped shut. "Please?"

Celeste looked down at him. "Will my blood help?"

Ethan's eyes flew open. He tried to laugh. "Elvish blood? I--I don't know."

"If I go out there to let them know you're alive, I'd rather you were conscious when I returned," Celeste said.

"I will be," Ethan whispered. "Go tell them--please--before they leave. You won't be able to get through the wards, otherwise--"

Celeste had already turned to the sink and selected a sharp knife from the block. She drew it across her wrist, drained the blood into a juice glass, then used her talent to close the wound.

Ethan watched, dumbstruck. "You're a Healer?"

"Not much of one, I'm afraid," Celeste said. "But enough of one to know when someone's on their last reserve of strength. Can you hold this?"

He managed with his left arm; his right had sustained a bullet wound and his hand didn't want to close around the glass.

She left him there, sitting on the floor, and walked down the driveway until the occupants of the car had noticed her presence.

The policeman approached. Celeste explained that she lived down the lane, but hadn't heard a thing. She was a sound sleeper, and her bedroom was in the back of the house. She'd noticed the flashing lights upon awakening, however, but she didn't have a phone to call anyone--

The policeman took down her statement, nodded to Andrew, and turned to walk back to his car.

To Andrew, Celeste said, "I don't believe we've met, but I know your name is Andrew. And the young lady in the passenger seat is Elizabeth, Ethan Walker's sister."

Andrew cursed. "Where is he?"

"Safe in my house," Celeste said. "But he's going to need more to drink-- I don't have the proper supplies to feed a vampire, and he's lost a lot of blood."

"You're the elf," Andrew said. "The weaver. Thomas said you were trustworthy--"

"I intend you no harm," Celeste said. "And I don't have a garage, so he'll have to stay in my house until dusk--"

"Who did this?" Andrew asked softly, staring at the bullet-ridden burned-out car.

"My guess would be Hunters," Celeste said. "Lucky for Ethan, they weren't using silver bullets."

Andrew cursed again. He turned to look at his car, then glanced at Celeste. "Would you mind if I sent one of the others back with you? If he'll last long enough, I'd rather wait until this is cleared away before I bring him blood--to not attract attention--"

"I gave him blood," Celeste began, and didn't completely miss Andrew's sudden look of horror. "He said he wasn't sure it would help. I don't know a lot about vampires--have I poisoned him?"

"No, not poison," Andrew said after a moment. "Shock, only; you're not bleeding; I see no bandages, no blood--"

"I have a small healing talent," Celeste said. "Not enough to heal his wounds, but enough to remove the bullets. I'm glad I haven't inadvertently poisoned him."

"So are we," Andrew said, and managed a smile. "And I've never known Thomas to give us false information. If he says you are trustworthy, then that's good enough for me."

"Thank you," Celeste said.

Andrew motioned towards the car. "Does he know his parents are dead?"

"He said they were dead before he escaped the wreck," Celeste said softly. "I'm sorry."

Andrew nodded and beckoned to Elizabeth. She walked towards them slowly, her eyes red from weeping.

"Please go with Celeste and keep Ethan company until I come back," Andrew said, and she stared at him, uncomprehending for a moment, and then a smile broke through her grief.

"He's not--"

They looked alike enough to be twins, but Celeste didn't want to pry. "Come with me," she said, and held out her hand. "I'm Celeste. And I apologize for not introducing myself before now."

Elizabeth prudently waited until they were past the wards before she asked, "Ethan is alive?"

"But badly hurt," Celeste said, and told her what she had witnessed. "I think he'll be fine, but he's lost a lot of blood."

Elizabeth nodded, but Celeste saw tears in her eyes. "I was supposed to go with them," she finally whispered. "But I didn't go. I was supposed to be in the car with them."

"I'm so sorry," Celeste said, and the girl--although a stranger--allowed her to draw her in close for a hug.

When they reached the back door and Celeste opened it, she found that Ethan had--somehow--managed to pull himself up onto one of the chairs around the kitchen table. He looked terrible even now, but Celeste thought she knew why he'd forced himself up off the floor; he was, after all, Head of the Walker Household now, and Heads of Households could not show much in the way of leadership from a rug on the floor.

The rug was literally *drenched* in blood. Elizabeth paled when she saw it, and then she saw Ethan, and for a few minutes, all she could do was clutch at her brother and cry. He met Celeste's gaze over his sister's head, half-helpless, half-resolute.

"Tea?" Celeste asked, because as far as she knew, vampires could drink tea.

"Please," Ethan said after a slight hesitation. And once Elizabeth had calmed down, and once the kettle was boiling, Celeste joined them both at the table.

"I spoke to Andrew," she said. "He told me he wanted to wait until the car had been taken away before he brought you something to drink."

Ethan's hands shook when he tried to pick up the mug. "That was smart of him," he said, his voice soft. "The police don't know the truth about us--they think we're some weird religious cult."

Celeste had not wished to push her blood upon him, although she didn't think he would refuse if she offered. And he obviously needed more blood. She set another juice glass in front of him silently. This one was full.

Elizabeth's breath caught in her throat. "You--you're *feeding* him?"

"I diluted it," Celeste said, and Ethan nodded, his eyes half-closed. He didn't speak again until he drained the cup dry.

"Thank you. You didn't have to do that, I would have been fine." But his voice shook as he spoke, and there were tears in his eyes again.

"Could you have fed him?" Celeste asked Elizabeth, who hesitated, then shook her head.

"Family blood," she said. "It's not--as edible to them."

"Andrew knew this?" Celeste asked. "And he didn't send someone else?"

"Andrew was the only one not blood-related to us in the car," Elizabeth said. "And the only one of us who knew how to drive."

Ethan let out a shaky breath. "Good. I'd hoped he wasn't intending to betray me."

"Andrew wouldn't--" Elizabeth began, but then she fell silent, considering.

"He could very easily come back by himself with poisoned blood for me to drink, having not told anyone I survived," Ethan said quietly. "It has happened before, when there was a change. A coup, I think the humans call it."

"And me? And Elizabeth?" Celeste asked.

Ethan just looked at her, his gaze tired now. "It happens," was all that he finally said. "But--" He sighed. "Despite the fact that I must think of it, I don't believe Andrew will betray us."

"And if he doesn't, then he'll be a trusted member of the family for the rest of his life," Elizabeth said, sounding much older than her apparent age.

"How old *are* you?" Celeste asked curiously.

"Fifteen," Ethan said.

"Fourteen," Elizabeth said.

"And you will be Head of Household despite the fact that you're not of age?" But she was attempting to fit human ages on a vampire, and she realized that just as Ethan said, "It's not the same. It's more like a succession, if you want to put a word to it."

"Hmm. Confusing, but not as confusing as kings and kingdoms in Faerie, I'd guess," Celeste said. "Are you in danger here?"

"If my aunt comes instead of Andrew, I know I'm safe," Ethan said. "If-- If someone else comes; even Andrew--" For a moment, she saw the child, not the sudden Head of Household, in his gaze.

"I'm not as easy to kill as you might think," Celeste said, but her words didn't seem to reassure him. "What about sunlight? Should I ward the house against it?"

"That would help, yes," Elizabeth said when Ethan didn't answer. She glanced at her brother, then back at Celeste, clearly unhappy.

"Ethan, you should lie down for a little while," Celeste said, and waited for him to protest that he had to stay awake. "In the library, perhaps--there's a couch there. It's not too uncomfortable."

"I can't walk that far," Ethan whispered, and the tears overflowed and spilled down his cheeks.

Elizabeth held him again, but this time, she was the strong one, comforting her brother as he had comforted her, just moments before.

Together, they helped him up and half-carried him into the library. A sheet on the couch would take care of any residual blood, although Celeste wished she had something for him to change into. He was asleep before they helped him lie down, completely and utterly exhausted.

And vulnerable, Celeste thought.

She left Elizabeth alone with her brother and went to see about the wards. Blocking sunlight wasn't difficult, just a bit tricky to tie in with the rest of the house wards, but she managed to make them work together nicely enough. Even so, it took the better part of an hour. By the time she returned to the library, Elizabeth had moved one of the chairs so she could sit beside Ethan, but she was not sitting in the chair. Instead, she was standing, looking out of the nearest window at something Celeste could not see.

"Trouble?" Celeste asked.

"The car's gone," Elizabeth said. "They took it away thirty minutes ago. And no one has come."

Celeste glanced at the clock, surprised to find that it was almost nine-thirty. "How long can he last like this?"

Elizabeth shrugged. "It's not that he won't last. It's that he won't be able to defend himself if someone attacks. He needs a lot more blood than you could possibly give him. And if Andrew decided to betray the family--"

"Ethan had a cell phone in his pocket," Celeste said. "Is there anyone we could call?"

"Aunt Dolly doesn't have a cell phone," Elizabeth said. "But we could call the house. If the news hasn't broken yet--"

"Then you can pretty much guess Andrew has betrayed you," Celeste said, and Elizabeth nodded. "What will he do if that happens?"

Elizabeth glanced at her uncertainly. "I'm not sure I should tell you," she said. "It's--family stuff."

Celeste retrieved Ethan's phone from where she'd put it on the kitchen table. No one had called, which seemed rather odd in itself. She handed the phone to Elizabeth, who hesitated, then dialed a number.

"The emergency number," she said. "Only to be used in an emergency. It only rings to one phone, and only certain people are allowed to answer it." She put the phone to her ear and listened to it ring.

"What if no one answers?" Celeste asked after a moment.

Elizabeth bit her lip. "Then--"

Someone picked up on the other end and barked a question. "Aunt Dolly, I--this is Elizabeth. Not Ethan."

"Can you make it so I can listen too?" Celeste asked. Elizabeth pressed a button, and Aunt Dolly's voice, crackling slightly, came through the phone's tiny speaker.

"...Ethan's phone?" She sounded ancient, but still strong; one of those women who refused to allow age to conquer her. "Elizabeth, where are you? And why do you have Ethan's phone?"

Elizabeth started to explain, but Celeste broke in when she hesitated. "Andrew was supposed to bring something back for Ethan to drink. He was shot six times. He lost a lot of blood."

"Andrew never came home," Aunt Dolly said. "Who are you?"

"My name is Celeste. I'm your neighbor," Celeste said. "What do you mean, he never came home?"

"Where are Scott and Erin?" Elizabeth asked. "They were in the car too."

"We don't know," Aunt Dolly said. And then, to Celeste, "My apologies-- you're the elf? The one who weaves? You rented the cottage on the edge of our property?"

"Yes," Celeste said.

"Dahlia Walker," Aunt Dolly said. "I let the children call me Dolly. And you have Ethan there with you? And he's alive?"

"Yes," Celeste said. "To both questions."

"Thomas said you were trustworthy," Aunt Dolly said, almost as if she were trying to decide for herself. "Okay. I'm going to send someone to you with blood for Ethan. Someone trustworthy."

"Who?" Elizabeth asked, half-panicked now, her eyes wide.

"Jack," Aunt Dolly said after a moment. "And Jill, of course. I apologize, Celeste; they're werewolves, but they hold loyalty to the family and the family alone."

"If I can open my home to vampires, then I can open my home to werewolves," Celeste said easily.

"I appreciate that," Aunt Dolly said. "They will be there to protect Ethan--by any means necessary. Do I have to explain?"

"No," Celeste said.

"You can deny them entry if you'd like, and they'll stay in the yard," Aunt Dolly said. "No one will fault you for that. I'll come as soon as I can, and then we'll be out of your hair--"

"I signed a two-year lease," Celeste said. "I'll admit--I should have introduced myself before now, but if I didn't wish to live next door to you, I wouldn't have signed the lease."

"You don't seem to be ignorant of vampires," Aunt Dolly said carefully. "Or--as prejudiced as some elves I've spoken with."

"I have a cousin who is fascinated by vampires," Celeste said, neglecting to mention that her cousin was also the king. "And the kingdom I'm from intersects the Richmond House's territory. We've had dealings--none good-- with them before, but I've been told they're a bit old-fashioned." From his place on the couch, Ethan croaked a laugh. Celeste hadn't realized he was awake.

"Old-fashioned," he murmured. "Bloodthirsty to both humans and their own kind. Not allies of ours."

"I would like to be your ally," Celeste said.

"Very well," Aunt Dolly said after a moment. "May I speak with Ethan? Privately?"

Elizabeth handed the phone to her brother and left the room. Celeste followed, but only after making sure Ethan was well and truly awake, because he had yet to open his eyes. And when she heard Aunt Dolly call her name, she walked back inside to find Ethan asleep again, or unconscious, and the phone on the floor.

"Turn off the speaker," Aunt Dolly said, and Celeste complied. "I don't want him to hear this," she said a moment later. "Can you go to another room?"

"Of course," Celeste said, and did just that.

"They just found Andrew, lying in a ditch a few miles away," Aunt Dolly said. "He's alive--for now. He's on his way to the hospital."

"Your people didn't find him, then," Celeste said, and watched as Elizabeth walked back into the library to sit with her brother.

"No. Some random person driving by saw something suspicious and stopped." She sighed. "I had my doubts Andrew was a traitor, but I would have had doubts about Scott and Erin as well. They're Elizabeth's age. Far too young for the Hunters to have them in hand. Unless they are working with children now."

"I'm sorry," Celeste said. "I wish we could have met under better circumstances."

"Me too," Aunt Dolly said. "Jack and Jill are on their way. Don't let anyone else inside. And--I wouldn't use this phone again. Do you have a landline?"

"No," Celeste said. "I don't. Or a car, or a garage."

"So he'll have to stay there until dusk," Aunt Dolly said. "Okay. You realize we'll owe you quite a large debt for this?"

"I know how it works," Celeste said. "And I know better than to protest."

"Of course you would," Aunt Dolly said without any rancor at all. "Keep him safe, please? He's my nephew."

"This house is not without protections," Celeste told her. "And I'll make sure he's alive to come home."

"Thank you," Aunt Dolly said. "I'll be there as soon as I can."

Celeste turned the phone off once the call had ended, just in case someone had been listening in. If they had, just the fact that Ethan was alive would spread quickly, and she wondered how long it would take for someone to make an attempt on his life, knowing he was wounded and weak and vulnerable.

She was--briefly--tempted to contact Nefir. But that might complicate things more than she wanted, not to mention the fact that she'd left Faerie to get away from her cousin and the sorrow of the past few years. Dredging it all up again to involve Nefir in this would not be a good idea.

A knock on the front door heralded the arrival of the werewolves--Jack and Jill--or so Celeste hoped. But when she went to answer the door, she saw only one person; a young human girl who looked like she'd been crying. Her clothes were dirty, her hair a mess, and she panted as if she'd run a long way.

"Elizabeth?" Celeste had no idea who she was or how she'd managed to get past the wards--unless, of course, she already knew the location of the cottage. "Could you come and tell me if you recognize this person?"

Elizabeth appeared from the library, peeked out the window, and gasped. "Erin!" She had her hand on the doorknob before Celeste stopped her.

"Your aunt said not to let anyone inside. I would assume that includes Erin."

Elizabeth dropped her hand. "Oh. But she-- She was in the car. With Andrew and Scott."

Outside, Erin knocked again, a little more desperate this time. She glanced behind her, too, as if expecting someone to be there, but the driveway was empty.

A phone rang. A cellphone, Celeste thought. Erin very nearly shrieked. She spun around as two people stepped out of the trees on either side of the cottage, then, when she recognized them, started babbling--hysterically--as if she expected them to strike first and ask questions later.

And they--Celeste had to assume this was Jack and Jill--didn't exactly exude an air of fierceness. They were both rather short; obviously twins; Jill wore her dark hair in a ponytail and Jack's hung loose down to his shoulders. They looked--more wild than fierce. But Erin seemed deathly afraid of them, and even Elizabeth looked wary.

"Your aunt said they were trustworthy," Celeste said, and noticed Jill carried a leather bag in one hand.

"They are. Fanatically trustworthy," Elizabeth said. "Um. You might want to open the door or they might kill her."

Celeste raised an eyebrow at that, but obeyed Elizabeth's instructions.

Erin nearly threw herself at the door as soon as it opened. "Please--please--I had nothing to do with this! I swear! I swear!" She burst into tears.

The tears seemed to puzzle the werewolves, who slowed. Jill glanced at her brother, then nodded to Celeste. "Truth?"

"I don't know," Celeste admitted. "But I'd like to find out, and leave her unharmed."

Jack's eyes never left Erin's quivering body. But he made no protest when Jill walked onto the porch and handed Celeste the bag. Instead, he followed his sister inside.

Elizabeth helped Erin up, and brought her inside. The girl stood there for a moment, staring at the werewolves, who seemed completely immune to her terror. And then, softly, she whispered, "Is Andrew alive?"

Jack's eyes flicked to Celeste, but only for a moment.

"He's on his way to the hospital," Celeste said.

Erin closed her eyes. "Thank goodness."

Elizabeth vanished into the library with the bag the werewolves had brought, leaving Celeste alone with the werewolves and Erin. They did not seem to be impressed by Erin's relief, but then again, perhaps they could smell a lie.

"What about Scott?" Erin asked, and this was almost an afterthought, as if she'd realized she should have been concerned for more than one person.

Jack had her against the wall, one hand around her throat, almost before Celeste realized he had moved.

"Scott was there too!" Erin squeaked, barely able to breathe. "He pushed me out of the car!"

"Let her speak," Celeste said, but after a glance at his sister, Jack ignored her.

"We need to hear what she has to say," Ethan said from the doorway.

He leaned heavily on Elizabeth, his face white with the effort, but he *was* standing, and he looked a little better.

Interestingly enough, instead of scenting him as wounded prey, Jack immediately released Erin and backed a few steps away from her. Erin turned towards the sound of Ethan's voice, saw him standing there in the doorway, gasped, swayed, and fainted.

Jill caught her before her head hit the floor. No one else had moved.

"Ethan?" Celeste asked, careful to keep her voice neutral. "I'd rather not have to clean up after a murder."

"We need to make sure she came alone," Ethan said, and Jill lowered Erin down to the floor, dusted off her hands, and left the house with her brother two steps behind her. "Elizabeth, help me over to a chair, please.

Celeste, do you have anything we can--" He briefly closed his eyes. "Secure her with? Just in case she is a traitor?"

"Rope?" Celeste asked. "Is she a wizard?"

"No," both Ethan and Elizabeth said at the same time.

"I'm a weaver," Celeste said. "I have plenty of yarn, rope, whatever you'd like."

"Nothing that breaks with human strength," Ethan said. "If you don't mind tying her hands and feet?"

Celeste tied her hands and feet with rug yarn, but not tightly enough to cut off her circulation. Ethan sat and watched from his place at the kitchen table, drinking from a mason jar that had, at one point, been sealed. There were five more like it; there had been eight packed carefully in the bag. As if Aunt Dolly hadn't quite known how much blood he'd need to replace, or how quickly he'd need to replace it.

After a little while, Erin awoke. She jerked awake, breathing hard, then seemed to realize she was tied and quieted, staring up at Ethan with wide eyes. "You're alive." Her voice was a croak. "I thought they had killed you."

"They didn't use silver bullets," Ethan said coldly. "Probably because I wasn't supposed to be with my parents last night. Elizabeth was supposed to go with them, not me."

Elizabeth had said something similar, earlier. And she sat beside her brother, pale and resolute, and asked, "Was I supposed to die too?"

"I don't know," Erin whispered. "I really and truly don't know."

"What *do* you know?" Ethan asked.

"Can I sit up?" Erin craned her head to look up at him. "I promise I won't try to escape. I'm not a wizard. I came back because I heard what Andrew said to Elizabeth. I thought--I thought you were keeping watch over Ethan's body, not that he was alive."

Without asking Ethan's permission, Celeste helped Erin sit up and lean back against the cabinets, so she could face Ethan and Elizabeth.

"You're an *elf,*" Erin said, almost in awe, as if she'd just noticed.

"Answer my question," Ethan said.

"There were Hunters at the drive-in last Tuesday," Erin said. "Scott, Pam, Jared, and I all went together. I saw the Hunters talking to Jared. He told me they knew who we were. We came home early. He said he was going to tell your parents, but--I don't know if he did."

"And where is Jared now?" Ethan asked.

"He was hiding in the back of the car," Erin whispered. "He had a gun. He pushed Andrew out into a ditch and Scott pushed *me* out and he t-told me to run--" Tears were running down her face now. "I heard the gun go off."

"Untie her, please," Ethan said, but Celeste was already in motion, untying the knots she'd made less than an hour before. Once Erin was free, she rubbed her wrists and ankles, and then, very quietly, said, "I'm sorry, Ethan. I thought--I believed him when he said he'd tell your parents. I'm the only one who saw him with the Hunters, and I didn't say anything and I should have."

"No," Ethan said. "This isn't your fault. You believed Jared and had no reason not to believe him. But for some reason, it seems he's betrayed us-- Celeste, my Aunt will need to know this."

"I don't have a phone," Celeste said. "And she told me not to use yours again."

Jack and Jill appeared, then, as if summoned. "She was alone," Jill said, looking curiously at Erin. "Have we determined her innocence?"

"We have," Ethan said. "We're looking for Jared. Do you know him?"

"I've smelled his scent before," Jill said, and Jack merely nodded. "But our duty is here, with you. As protection."

"And if I ask you to track Erin's scent back to where she was pushed from the car to make sure Scott isn't lying in a ditch bleeding to death?" Ethan asked.

"And if Jared shows up here and tries to kill you?" Jill countered. "What then?"

"You could split up," Celeste suggested, but as soon as she said it, she realized how impossible that would be. The werewolves were a team; a pair. They worked in tandem, together. "Never mind."

Jack smiled, briefly, and nodded, as if in agreement.

"There is someone we could call," Jill said.

"Who?" Ethan asked.

For the first time, Jack spoke. "William." His gaze was almost--defiant.

Ethan hesitated, but only for a moment. "Just this once."

Jack was outside almost before he finished speaking. Celeste watched him shift shape--it was something she'd never forget; a subtle darkening in the air, almost masking his shape, and then, a wolf--and then he howled. Long and loud and piercing.

Only five minutes later, another wolf appeared. Jack and the other wolf seemed to converse for a moment, and then the second wolf loped off into the trees, presumably following Erin's scent.

Jack shifted shape and walked back into the kitchen.

"How long has he been in the area?" Ethan asked. "I thought--"

"You don't know the whole story," Jill said, interrupting him. "And neither did your parents. If William has his way, you'll never know. But he'll do this--for you, because of what happened this morning, and because your parents did not deserve to die like that."

"He hates Hunters more," Jack explained.

"That's--slightly reassuring," Ethan said neutrally. "I won't forget that he was willing to help." He glanced at Celeste and almost smiled. "And I'm willing to forget how quickly he came here--"

Jack looked surprised. Jill merely nodded. "Thank you."

Elizabeth did not look happy about this, but Celeste supposed she didn't have much of a choice now that Ethan was Head of Household. She had to wonder, though, what William had done to be banished, or exiled; the vampires did not seem the type to resort to exile when they held so much power otherwise.

"May I--" Erin ducked her head, embarrassed. "May I use your bathroom?"

"Sure," Celeste said. "Follow me." She led the girl down the hallway to the bathroom, then returned to the kitchen. Both Jack and Jill were staring now, on alert, as if they had sensed something wrong.

And then Ethan lurched to his feet. Not quite steady; not quite healed, but he pushed away from the table and almost fell the second he tried to stand on his own. "Enough!" He nearly shouted the word. "Enough bloodshed for one day! Stop her--"

The two werewolves vanished down the hall. They tore open the door; Celeste supposed she was lucky it didn't have a lock, and she heard Erin's shrill scream. Ethan swayed where he stood, but remained standing, holding onto the table for support, his eyes almost closed.

Elizabeth had not moved. She stared at her clenched hands fixedly, only the tears on her cheeks evidence to the fact that her friend had evidently decided to attempt suicide. But why?

"Because she failed the Family," Ethan whispered, his voice barely audible. "Or feels that she does, even though I absolved her of blame." He opened his eyes. "Is she hurt?"

"Nothing that a bandage won't fix," Jill said, her voice very nearly concerned. "Her head, though, is another matter."

"Her head?" Celeste murmured.

"Her mind," Elizabeth whispered.

"It's been a hard day for everyone," Celeste said, and watched as Jack and Jill gently maneuvered Erin out of the bathroom and down the hall again. The girl's wrist was wrapped with a hand towel; without comment, Celeste took her arm and set her talent to work at healing the wound.

Ethan did not sit down again. He stayed standing, watching Celeste; watching Erin, his face completely devoid of emotion. Erin couldn't stop crying, but she wasn't sobbing now, just leaking tears; she made no move to wipe them away. Her eyes were tightly closed, her face blotchy and red. And after a long while, she cried herself to sleep, huddled in Celeste's arms.

Ethan finally seemed to realize he was still standing. He tried to take a step backwards, but his legs--locked in one position for so long--almost collapsed under him. Elizabeth caught one arm, and Jack caught the other; together they helped him back to the chair.

"If one of you watches over her, she can sleep on the couch in the library," Celeste said softly, and Jill lifted Erin up without any apparent effort to carry her away. "She'll sleep for a while," she added, and Ethan nodded, his eyes closed again.

"You should rest," Elizabeth told him, and poured him another glass of blood. "Or drink. Take your pick."

"I'll drink," Ethan said, and did just that, steadily, and for every cup Elizabeth poured, he looked less likely to fall over the next time he tried to stand.

Hours passed. Celeste made lunch; she had no idea what werewolves ate, but they didn't seem interested in her offering, so she left them to their own devices. After a little while, Elizabeth helped Ethan into the weaving room and onto the upholstered chair; it wasn't quite as comfortable as the couch, but he didn't seem to mind, and Celeste was left without much of anything to do.

So she sat down at her loom and wove. The steady *thunk* of the beater bar soothed both mind and spirit, and Ethan did not stir at the sound, so she continued until late afternoon when Jack stepped out onto the front porch to greet William's return.

She didn't follow him, but she set the shuttle aside and walked to the window nonetheless.

William didn't shift shape again, but this time, Jack stayed in human form. Still, it seemed they had no trouble conversing; and from the look on Jack's face, the news was either tragic or inconclusive.

And then, Celeste saw an old woman walking down the driveway, long before either werewolf noticed. Jack's head snapped up, guilty; William turned to face her, wary. And Dahlia Walker--Aunt Dolly--stopped short when she saw them both, said something Celeste could not hear, and motioned towards the cottage with her cane.

Celeste thought that Jack said Ethan's name. Aunt Dolly didn't care; she motioned again towards the cottage, angrily now.

"Jill?" Celeste did not raise her voice for fear of waking Ethan. "I think your brother needs your voice. I'll sit with Erin."

"No need," Elizabeth said, and hurried into the library as Jill emerged. "I'll sit with her."

Celeste followed Jill to the front door. When she opened it, Jack turned and William whined; Aunt Dolly snapped, "Don't think I can't speak werewolf, William," and he stared at her in surprise. "Inside, please. All of you. If Ethan truly knows about this, then I'm not going to go against him, but I don't think it was a good idea."

"No phone, a missing young man, and a gunshot?" Celeste asked from the porch. "I'm surprised. We had no way to contact you; you told me not to use Ethan's phone again. And Erin said--"

Aunt Dolly held up her hands. "Wait. Inside, please. These are fabulous wards, but even so." When William would have slunk away, she pointed the tip of her cane at him. "You too."

"He would prefer--" Jack began, almost helplessly.

"No," Jill said before Aunt Dolly could speak. "We'll share information, together, so no one is misinformed. We have information you do not, Aunt. And we asked for William's help because to delay any longer might have meant the loss of a life--a member of the Family. And we've lost enough today."

Aunt Dolly nodded. "Very well." She walked the rest of the way to the porch steps, then smiled up at Celeste. "I'm pleased to meet you, although I wish we'd met under better circumstances."

"Me too," Celeste said. "Please, come inside."

There weren't enough chairs for everyone to sit at the kitchen table, but Ethan was back in his customary seat by the time everyone followed Celeste inside. The werewolves took refuge in the corner near the stove, all three of them together, Jack and Jill on either side of William, who still had not shifted shape.

Aunt Dolly stopped short when she saw Ethan sitting at the table. To Celeste's eyes, he looked a lot better than before, but it must have been a shock nonetheless to see her nephew covered in blood.

"I should have brought you a change of clothes," she said, almost awkwardly.

Ethan smiled. "It's nice to see you too, Aunt Dolly."

"I'm sorry, Ethan," the old woman said, her voice soft.

Ethan nodded and glanced away from her, as if he did not trust his emotions just yet. After a moment of silence, he said, "I would be satisfied to hear William's account from Jack's lips. That is, if he has something to report?"

"Scott is dead," Jack said simply. "William followed the car as far as he could before the trail was too muddy to track."

Ethan nodded, unsurprised. "You may go," he said to William. "Thank you again."

William cast a wary glance at Aunt Dolly, who hesitated, then said, "I would prefer to hear it from William's own lips. No offense, Jack."

William growled. Jack gasped.

"Unless you wish to break the spell, that's quite impossible," Jill said quietly.

"A spell?" Celeste asked. "Preventing him from shifting shape?"

"Punishment," Aunt Dolly said, sounding as if she wished Celeste was not in the room. "You mentioned Erin? She's here?"

"She tried to cut her wrists in my bathroom," Celeste said, and saw Ethan's barely perceptible wince.

Aunt Dolly looked at Ethan, then transferred her gaze to Celeste. "I see. Where is she now?"

"Elizabeth is sitting with her," Ethan said. "She feels she failed us by not reporting that she saw Jared speaking with a group of Hunters at the drive-in last week."

"And the reason why she didn't report it?" Aunt Dolly asked.

"Jared assured her he had every intention of informing my parents of their presence," Ethan said. "And she believed him."

"Of course she believed him," Aunt Dolly murmured. "She had no reason not to believe him, poor child." She looked at William for a long minute, considering. He had not moved after her first protest, but Celeste saw something in his gaze now, something she doubted either Aunt Dolly or Ethan could miss.

"I had nothing to do with his punishment," Ethan said, his voice completely neutral. A smile flickered across Jack's lips at his words. "If you wish to hear his report in his own voice--and I would have to insist on a *human* voice, since I don't speak werewolf--then you'll have to remove the spell." He paused. "And if you remove it, it's gone for good. But I will leave that decision up to you."

Aunt Dolly opened her mouth to reply, then closed it again. For a moment, the silence in the room was complete, save for the ticking of the clock and the hum of the fridge. "You assume I had a hand in his punishment," she finally said. "I did not."

"Who did?" Celeste asked.

"A dozen years ago," Ethan said. "I was three years old. All I remember are the stories."

William whined, then caught himself, as if he hadn't wanted to make a sound.

"I would like to know the real story," Ethan said. "Since I know all of the others."

"Perhaps this is not the right day for the telling of stories," Aunt Dolly began.

"Ethan's stuck here until dusk," Celeste pointed out. "And that's a few hours yet."

"Hmm." Aunt Dolly looked around the room. "I can see I've been outvoted. William? What say you to this?"

William looked at Jack, then Jill. Jack shook his head and pursed his lips, obviously disapproving; Jill said, gently, "Are you certain? Because I doubt you'll get this opportunity again."

"He says that he didn't agree to help for this type of payment," Jack said abruptly, and folded his arms against his chest.

"Who are you protecting?" Celeste asked, because that was the only explanation that made sense. She wasn't sure how a wolf could look surprised, but William managed it, and even forgot himself enough to take a few steps backwards, as if to escape the question before anyone could consider the ramifications of an answer. "Or who are you afraid of?"

"Oh," Ethan said, and carefully stood up. He didn't wobble quite as much this time; the blood had helped. "But is your loyalty to the person you're afraid of or to the family? Because it *has* been twelve years. And that's a long time to stay silent."

"Who cast the spell?" Celeste asked.

"I don't know," Ethan said. "Aunt Dolly?"

"The only thing I know about this is the spell was his punishment, or so we were told. Or did she buy your silence with the spell, William?" Aunt Dolly took a step towards him and he growled. "It's unlikely she'll know you're free; this house is well-protected and well-warded."

"'She'?" Ethan asked.

Before Aunt Dolly could reply, Jack said, quickly, "Please don't speak her name. William says he only recently escaped from her, and he doesn't want to go back."

"Ah," Aunt Dolly said. "I see. May we say Jared's mother instead?" She raised an eyebrow at Ethan. "The very same Jared who has--evidently--murdered one of our family, and attempted the lives of two others, if Andrew still lives?"

Celeste saw Elizabeth standing in the doorway of the library, listening. She motioned her forward, intending to watch over Erin herself, but Elizabeth shook her head. "No, I'll stay here. I can hear you just fine."

"This was a coup attempt, wasn't it?" Ethan asked unhappily. "Not just Hunters."

"She was not in the House when I left," Aunt Dolly said. "I've suspected her motives for a while now. Your parents knew my suspicions, but we had no cause to act. But you two--you should have told someone when you found William."

"Vampire or human?" Celeste asked.

"Human," Ethan murmured. "When you *found* William? He did not seek you out? You found him where?" To Celeste, he said, "Not all of the family live together. Jared's mother has a house in town. It's isolated. We don't visit. How long did she keep you there?"

Jack glanced at his sister before replying. "The last question first. The whole time. Twelve years. We found him in the forest. He swore us to secrecy. We helped him get stronger."

"He--" Jill made a face, as if she'd tasted something sour. "He was wearing a *collar*."

It would be, of course, a terrible insult to a werewolf, Celeste thought. She held out her hand. "Were you hurt? I have a small talent for healing, if you would allow me to touch you, William."

"Who can I trust, then?" Ethan asked his aunt, his voice soft, but firm.

"Well, me," Aunt Dolly said. "And despite the fact that Jack and Jill sheltered William without our knowledge, I'm fairly certain they are still trustworthy."

"You have no need to question our loyalty," Jill said firmly.

"In the advent that this was a coup attempt, I've already contacted those I know who are loyal," Aunt Dolly said. "You will not be without a guard, at home, until this is over."

"We heal fast," Jack said to Celeste. "When given the chance to heal."

Celeste nodded and dropped her hand. "I'm sorry. No one deserves to be a slave to someone else, no matter what the crime."

Ethan sighed and sat down again. Put his head in his hands. And looked so *young* for a moment that Celeste wondered how he would manage *without* protection. Was he a wizard? Who held the House wards?

Aunt Dolly hesitated. "Now is not the time to show weakness," she said. "If you intend to hold this House, then you *must* be strong, Ethan."

"I was shot six times this morning," Ethan muttered through his hands. "My parents were murdered. There was a coup attempt that seems to be still ongoing. Scott is dead; Andrew may be yet. Erin might never be the same again, and I can't go home until the sun sets." He uncovered his face and glared at his aunt. "And you're telling me I need to be *strong*?"

"Don't think I wouldn't rather mourn my brother's death," Aunt Dolly said sharply. "But time for mourning will be after we've stopped the carnage. Jack; Jill; you are still charged with keeping Ethan safe. I don't want you to let him leave your sight. Elizabeth, your duty is to Erin. Don't allow her to harm herself again."

"Who holds the House wards?" Ethan asked abruptly.

"I do," Aunt Dolly said. "We'll have to do something about that later; I'm not getting any younger, and it's best to have more than one person involved. There's a marked lack of wizards in the Household; we'll have to do something about that as well."

"What, do you advertise for wizards or something?" Celeste asked, intrigued.

"There's enough of a Hunter presence, and enough deaths that some Houses vanish entirely, and those who remain are integrated in other Houses. Or they become--houseless, and travel between places until they find a home." Ethan uncovered his face and raised his head. "William, I'm sorry, but I need to know what you know. I need to know the true story. If you hold any loyalty to me or the House, I am asking for it now. And I will repay you for your loyalty."

William stared at him for a moment, then stepped away from Jack and Jill, towards Aunt Dolly. His entire posture screamed reluctance; he was more afraid of Jared's mother than of Ethan. Or was it something else entirely? After a dozen years in the shape of a wolf--

"Perhaps there shouldn't be an audience for this," Aunt Dolly said. "May we go somewhere private, Celeste? And William might need clothing--do you have anything he would be able to wear?"

"It depends--how tall is he?" Celeste asked. "Ethan, I may have a shirt you could wear; I have some clothes to cut up for rugs in the closet. But there's not a great selection." She'd forgotten about the bag of clothes; they'd been stuffed in the back of the closet since she moved.

"Why don't we see what we can find?" Ethan suggested, his gaze on William.

Aunt Dolly opened her mouth, perhaps to suggest Ethan stay behind as well, but he was already on his feet, and already walking--without holding onto the table for balance--towards the weaving room. And after a glance at Aunt Dolly, William followed him.

"A pair of scissors too, perhaps?" Aunt Dolly asked.

"On the table," Celeste said.

Both Jack and Jill followed Ethan into the weaving room as well. Celeste heard him question them, heard Jill reply, "Orders," and when they didn't emerge, Aunt Dolly followed them inside and closed the door.

Celeste heard low voices from the living room. Elizabeth was gone from the doorway; she'd have to assume Erin was awake. She stood in the doorway for a moment until they noticed her; Erin still lay on the couch, pale and listless, her eyes dull. Elizabeth was holding her hand.

"Erin, would you like something to eat or drink?" Celeste asked.

"Tea?" Elizabeth suggested when Erin didn't answer.

"Tea it is, then," Celeste said, and walked back into the kitchen, glad to have something to do.

Thirty minutes later, Ethan emerged, wearing a t-shirt that was only a little too big (with Jack as his silent shadow), and asked for soap and water. Celeste directed him to the bathroom, but before he returned, Aunt Dolly poked her head out of the weaving room and said, "Perhaps it would be better if we reconvened into the bathroom?"

Celeste joined Erin and Elizabeth in the living room, to give William more privacy. She heard them go past; neither Erin nor Elizabeth seemed inclined to peek, and she heard the shower start a moment later. In fact, Erin seemed disinclined to speak at all, although she smiled once, a small, sad smile that broke Celeste's heart.

When she heard them in the kitchen, she waited for a minute before Ethan called her name, not wanting to intrude. And when she joined them, she saw that William had every right for his hesitation.

He was cadaverously thin, resembling Jack and Jill quite strongly, although he seemed older, in both manner and appearance. His hair was cut short--shorter than Jack's, at least, but it was still slightly ragged. Celeste had to assume that twelve years of growth had been newly cut away.

He sat at the table as if he'd forgotten how to sit at a table, mimicking Ethan's posture and position on the chair. They'd found clothes for him to wear--another black t-shirt, which swamped his thin frame, and a pair of cotton pants that were far too long, but at least they gave him some dignity.

There was a glass of water sitting in front of him, but he made no move to pick it up. Celeste had to wonder if he'd remember how to drink, after twelve years as a wolf. Could he even *speak?*

Evidently, Ethan had the same reservations. "I won't force you to talk," he said. "If you would prefer Jack to speak for you--"

William opened his mouth. "I--I would like to speak for myself." His voice was rusty from disuse, but it was a voice, most definitely. "I never lost my loyalty to the family. I won't say I did not deserve punishment for what I did--"

"What did you do?" Ethan asked.

William closed his eyes. Took a breath. "Caused the death of one of your cousins. A vampire. Her name was Ginger. She was six years old."

"And how did Jared's mother get involved in your punishment?" Aunt Dolly asked.

"She's the one who found us," William said. "Or, me, I guess. When I woke up, she told me what had happened, and she told me she'd been put in charge of my punishment. And she said--"

"Wait, *she* told you what had happened?" Ethan asked.

"I have no memory of it," William said. "I still don't, although I've tried. The last thing I remember is leading her to a barn, because it was almost dawn. Her two older brothers had asked me to take her to safety. There were Hunters--"

"How old were you twelve years ago?" Celeste asked.

William had to think for a moment. "Eleven."

"A child," Celeste said. "And no one questioned your punishment?"

"Twelve years ago, werewolves weren't as trusted," Jill said. "And it's not like we had parents."

"What happened to your parents?" Celeste asked. "It's obvious you're related--"

"William is our older brother," Jack said. "Jill and I are twins. Our parents were killed by Hunters soon after we were born."

Aunt Dolly said, "Twelve years ago, I was not living here. I found out about all of this when I returned. And by that time, William had vanished, Ginger's brothers were dead, and all that was left were the stories."

"I've heard the stories," William whispered, his eyes still closed.

"I haven't," Celeste said.

"Take your pick," William said. "Either I savagely attacked her, or I gave her up to the Hunters to save my own skin. Or I led her into the barn and set fire to it to cover up some secret thing I did to her body after I strangled her." He opened his eyes. "I'm fairly sure that one's not true. The barn is still standing. I've been there. And werewolves don't tend to strangle their prey."

"Or you raped and murdered her and tried to make it look like the Hunters had found your hiding place," Ethan said. "That's the one I heard."

"There was talk when I returned that we should not welcome werewolves into the Household any longer," Aunt Dolly said. "That they couldn't be trusted. That even the children were demons in disguise."

"And you don't remember anything," Celeste said to William, who shook his head.

"I remember walking into the barn with her and looking up at the ceiling to make sure there was enough cover from the sun," he said. "And the next thing I remember was waking up in *her* house. And that's where I spent the next twelve years."

"How did you escape?" Ethan asked.

"She thought I was dead," William said. "I hope she still thinks I am dead. I might have *been* dead; I don't know. But Jack and Jill found me, and nursed me back to health, and I've been living in the forest ever since."

"Not long," Celeste guessed.

"Since winter," William said. "There was snow on the ground when I opened my eyes."

A few months, then, and not much more. And he looked as if he'd come back from the brink of death; he was much too thin, if Jack and Jill were any indication of how he should have looked.

"Perhaps we can find out the truth," Ethan said. "If you wish to know it, of course."

"Of course I want to know it," William said, as if there could be any question. "I'd like to know what happened. I'd like to know if I'm--" He looked down at his hands. "If I'm a monster."

"How old would Jared have been twelve years ago?" Ethan asked.

"Around the same age," Aunt Dolly replied.

"But he's human," William said, as if believing a human could be capable of such violence was too extraordinary to even consider.

"Humans can be very cruel," Ethan said. "Especially children. Did Jared know you were a prisoner?"

"Jared--" William shuddered. "Yes. He knew."

"Does it still seem surprising that he could have been involved?" Aunt Dolly asked.

"No," William whispered. "No, not at all."

"We'll find the truth," Ethan said. "And I think, even if you *were* guilty, you've suffered enough."

"Thank you," William said. "You won't regret accepting my loyalty."

"How will we ensure they don't succeed?" Ethan asked. "I don't want to spend the rest of my life looking over my shoulder." He scowled when his aunt would have spoken. "And don't tell me it comes with the territory."

"It does, truthfully," Celeste said. "But it's not as hard to bear if you surround yourself with those you trust."

"You sound as if you speak from experience," Ethan said slowly.

"I do." Celeste remembered how adamant Nefir had been that she stay within the kingdom--in safety. "Granted, elves don't have as many coup attempts, or Hunters, but some of us seem to thrive on betrayal." Before they could ask, she said, "My cousin Nefir is king where I'm from. We had a--disagreement. I thought it best if I left for a little while."

"How long have you been gone?" Aunt Dolly asked.

"Nearly twenty years," Celeste said. "He still wants me to come back. I will, eventually, but not for a little while yet."

"You don't look old enough to have been gone nearly twenty years," William said, surprised.

"Elves age even slower than vampires, or so I've been told," Celeste said. "Nefir has a bit of a fascination with vampires."

"An interesting hobby for a king to have," Ethan commented. "I assume this is the cousin you spoke of before?"

"The very same," Celeste said. "I'm sure he'd love to meet you. But I'm also certain he'd never leave you alone, so maybe that's not a good idea. I blame his fascination on the Richmonds; they, ah, tend to chain their unwanted family members to trees right outside the Veil and leave them for the dawn. Nefir saved one of them once."

"They are not a valid example of a vampire family," Ethan said. "Is Erin awake? I'd like to speak with her."

"She was awake, but she hasn't spoken," Celeste said. "Elizabeth?"

Elizabeth appeared in the doorway and shook her head. "Asleep again."

"I think it might be best if I speak to her while she's asleep," Ethan said, and stood up. "You can leave us alone. I won't harm her."

Elizabeth stepped out of the room, frowning slightly. Ethan vanished inside. He had no trouble walking now, Celeste noted; save for the blood on his pants, she would never have guessed he'd been wounded.

"How can he speak to her while she's asleep?" she asked, when no one volunteered the information.

"It's something they can do," Jill said. "We can't."

"In some families, it's how they control their members," Aunt Dolly said. "Not this one, however." Louder, she said, "Ethan, all I have to do is make one call."

It took almost fifteen minutes for Ethan to respond. "Make the call." He appeared in the doorway, looking both tired and disgusted. "I have enough. And they've been inside her mind already. That's proof enough for me."

"That means a vampire's involved," Aunt Dolly said.

"And I know who it is," Ethan said, but he did not name the vampire. "Make the call. The vampire isn't going anywhere just yet. The humans, however--"

"I'll have to speak her name," Aunt Dolly said to William, who nodded. She took a cell phone from her pocket and dialed a number. She gave no instructions, but only said two names: Jared and Anita Cummings. "And now we wait."

"What do you do to traitors?" Celeste asked.

"We'll see after they're in custody," Ethan said. "Aunt Dolly, give them one other name."

Aunt Dolly took out her phone again. When Ethan didn't speak, she looked at him, then said, "You might as well say it. It's not going to get any more palatable."

"Bir--Birdie Walker," Ethan whispered, sounding as if he spoke the words through a throat full of sand. "Bernadette."

"You're certain," Aunt Dolly said sharply. "Absolutely certain."

"There's no way to hide a presence in someone's mind," Ethan said. "Especially a human's mind. She was there. She tried to make Erin forget she saw Jared speaking with the Hunters. She succeeded, but sometimes a great shock will knock things loose again. And Erin has had a big shock."

"Who is Birdie Walker?" Celeste asked.

"A very close cousin," Elizabeth said from where she sat in Ethan's seat, stunned. "Why would she do something like this?"

"She was in charge of warding the House vehicles," Aunt Dolly said.

"But why would a vampire be in league with the Hunters?" Celeste asked.

"Sometimes the Hunters will allow the House to remain, if the worst members--their words--are killed," Ethan said. "That happened to the Alsepts a few years ago. I heard Mom and Dad talking about it."

Elizabeth's face crumpled. Ethan didn't seem to notice, but Celeste thought he realized what he had said, because he turned away from them with his arms folded, his shoulders stiff and unyielding.

"If Birdie is a traitor, then who else?" Jill asked sensibly.

"Who else," Ethan echoed, almost hopelessly. "Why? Why would she do this? Jared and his mother are human; I can almost believe their betrayal. But Birdie? Why?"

"As you said, sometimes the Hunters bargain," Aunt Dolly said. "That could be why. They might--" Her phone rang; shrill in the sudden silence. William's gaze was on Ethan, who had not turned around.

Aunt Dolly answered the phone before it could ring again. She listened for a moment, then mentioned Birdie's name. Listened again. "Yes. I'll tell him," she murmured, but the werewolves must have been able to hear, because they obviously already knew.

"They have Anita in custody," Aunt Dolly said. "She was in her home, alone. They think they know where Jared is headed. And Birdie--"

"She's dead, isn't she?" Ethan asked before she could speak.

"She left you a note," Aunt Dolly said. "They haven't read it. They will keep it for you to read." And then, softer, "It was the honorable thing to do, since she knew we would discover her betrayal."

"Honorable," Ethan whispered, and shook his head. "Cowardly. I may need that note before nightfall."

"Why?" Elizabeth asked.

Ethan turned around. "We're vulnerable now," he said. "The Hunters are closing in. They may have plans to attack us, and what better night than tonight? When everything is in chaos?" He started to say something else, but then he stopped. And, wonderingly, said, "Elizabeth, you were supposed to be in the car with Mom and Dad. It was a last minute change that I went with them."

Elizabeth nodded. "That's true."

"Why didn't you go?" Ethan asked.

"I wasn't feeling well," Elizabeth said. "I thought it might have been something I ate, but it went away about an hour after you left."

"If I had been killed along with our parents, you would have been head of Household," Ethan said. "It was a fluke, nothing more, that the Hunters did not have silver bullets. Maybe they weren't notified of the change--"

"Maybe *you* were supposed to become Head of Household," Celeste said. "And if Elizabeth was dead along with your parents, you would be the last in the direct line of Walkers or something like that?"

Aunt Dolly smiled faintly. "Something like that, yes."

"And then, knowing you would be vulnerable, the Hunters attack, and you are killed--" Celeste didn't like this line of thought, but she couldn't see any way around it. "They didn't count on two things, if this is true."

"What two things?" Aunt Dolly asked.

"Three things, really," Celeste said. "One, I found you before dawn. Two, Elizabeth didn't go with your parents. You're both alive. And three, William's return from the dead."

Ethan stared at her. "All of this, according to their plan?"

"If I hadn't seen you, you would have burned to death," Celeste said. "And they wouldn't have known about me; I've barely left the cottage since I arrived, and they'd have nowhere to look. I'm an elf. It's not like I have a driver's license or birth certificate or an actual official presence in the Human World."

"Granted," Aunt Dolly said. "But now that this has happened--if this was part of their plan, then what?"

"I'd be very interested in who asked about Ethan after they left last night," Celeste said. "And who was very surprised to find out he's alive now."

"This might not be over," Ethan said. "That's what you're saying."

"I think calling a family meeting might not be a bad idea," Celeste said. "If you do such things."

Ethan hesitated. "Would you come to it?"

"If you think it would be helpful," Celeste said. "And if no one here minds."

"Ethan is Head of Household now," Aunt Dolly said. "Even if we minded, it wouldn't matter."

Celeste remembered that she'd waited until Ethan himself suggested it before breaking the spell over William to allow him to shift shape. "Then I will go."

"Thank you," Ethan said. "Tonight, I think. To quickly put this to rest."

"There's a couple of hours until dusk," Celeste said. "What will you do until then?"

Ethan glanced back at his aunt. "Mourn," he said softly. "I would like a little time alone. *Truly* alone," he said when Jack made as if to follow him. "I'll still be in the house. You shouldn't have to worry." Before anyone could speak, he walked into the library and closed the door behind him.

"Alone with a compromised human?" Jill murmured, but made no move to stop him.

Celeste shook her head. "I'm going to assume that's not a good idea," she said, and opened the library door.

Ethan stood in front of the window, staring out. Erin was still asleep on the couch. When she opened the door, he turned, angry that his order had not been kept. And then he saw it was Celeste, and the anger drained away.

His cheeks were wet with tears.

"They weren't quite sure that leaving you alone with a compromised human was a good idea, but none of them wished to go against your order," Celeste said. "Maybe you should mourn in the weaving room instead? We can lock the connecting door, and your wolves can watch over Erin."

Ethan nodded, not speaking, as if he couldn't quite trust his voice. Celeste opened the connecting door and led him into the weaving room again; her favorite room in the entire house.

He sat down in the chair, then stood and walked over to the loom. "If you mess up my blanket, I may have to revoke my invitation," Celeste said, not quite kidding. He glanced up at her, his smile not quite reaching his eyes.

"Can I watch you weave?" He hesitated. "When I was asleep, before, I heard you, but I wasn't awake to watch."

"Let me tell them where you are first, okay?" Celeste asked.

He nodded. Sat down on the bench beside the loom, looking a bit lost now, and far too young to be Head of any House at all.

Celeste informed the others that Ethan was in the weaving room and did not wish to be disturbed. And then she joined him--at least no one commented on *that*--and she sat down in front of the loom and began to weave.

As she wove, she explained the various steps, and while he didn't say much, he seemed interested enough so that when she offered him the shuttle, he didn't immediately refuse to try.

"I'm not certain--" he began.

"You can't really hurt it," Celeste said. "That was a joke."

"I know," Ethan said. "But I don't know what I'm doing."

"You've watched me long enough to know the basics," Celeste said. "The hard work has been done already."

Ethan took the shuttle from her hand and looked down at it. "That's not what I meant, exactly--"

"I know," Celeste said.

"I'm only fifteen years old," Ethan whispered. He glanced up at her, vulnerable now that he was away from the others. "I don't have a clue what I'm supposed to do. Put them to death? Kill them myself? They would have been very happy to kill me, or Elizabeth--"

"They'll expect you to sentence the traitors to death," Celeste said. "Won't they? What would your parents have done?"

"Ah," Ethan said, and scooted onto the bench in front of the loom. "My parents. I miss my parents." He hesitated, then correctly pressed the treadles to maintain the pattern on the cloth in front of him. Moving the shuttle through the raised shed, pulling the beater bar towards him after each pass.

"I'm sure you do," Celeste said, her voice soft.

He continued weaving for a moment, then stopped, staring down at the cloth. "We don't--we don't *do* things like this. Create. A blanket from strands of yarn. It's so soft."

"Wool," Celeste said. "With a little cashmere added."

He added a bit more, working slowly but steadily, not missing a beat. After a few minutes, he said, "If the traitors were--" He stopped. "If the family is this piece of cloth, then the traitors were scissors, tearing it to pieces. It's up to me to weave it back together again."

"It might not look the same," Celeste said, approving of his analogy.

"But it will be whole," Ethan said. And then, thoughtfully, "And it might be stronger."

"That's true," Celeste said.

Ethan took a deep breath. "I know what I need to do now." He paused. Wove another inch. "It's not something I want to do, or something I will enjoy. But it's necessary."

"I think my cousin would be proud," Celeste said, and watched as he wove, inch by inch, until the sun had set and the world outside was lost to darkness.

At full dark, a small SUV drove down Celeste's driveway and waited outside. Ethan named the young man who drove as Peter; Aunt Dolly deemed him trustworthy. She sat up front, with Erin, who walked as if drugged, still not speaking. The werewolves piled in the back, leaving Ethan, Elizabeth, and Celeste to the middle.

It was only a mile or so down the road to the gates that led to the Walker compound, but every single person in the car was on edge--save, perhaps, for Ethan, who seemed strangely calm. He had not discussed what he intended to do about the traitors, and no one had asked. But as they drove down the gravel driveway, he said, "I would like to see Birdie's note. And then I'd like to call a family meeting."

"Of course," Aunt Dolly said. "Might I ask what you intend to do?"

"The Hunters wished to kill vampires," Ethan said, and he wasn't even looking at them now; he stared out the window, watching the trees go by.

"For some reason, Birdie, Jared, and his mother intended to help them. I'm intending to give the Hunters what they wanted."

"But Jared and his mother are human," Jill said slowly.

William laughed aloud, but did not explain.

"Oh, very good," Aunt Dolly said. "I think that will get the point across quite nicely."

"I thought it might," Ethan said.

The SUV pulled up to a perfectly normal looking ranch-style house, albeit one that had been added to over the years, because it seemed a lot larger than the original structure would have warranted. Peter pulled the car into the garage, and everyone waited until the door had closed before exiting.

They were met by four unsmiling men and one woman--all much older than Ethan, all presumably loyal. Celeste was amused to discover that her presence gave them pause; but they looked to Ethan for an explanation, not his aunt.

"I give Celeste family privileges," Ethan said. "She saved my life."

And that seemed to be the end of it, because they asked no other questions. Two of them half-carried Erin into the house and handed her over to another woman with short gray hair who hurried her away.

A younger woman--and Celeste thought this one was a vampire--handed Ethan an envelope, even before he stepped into the house. He thanked her, named her as Aurora, and, with Jack and Jill as his shadows, walked into the house.

There were others now, watching from doorways; Celeste ended up beside William, who looked extremely uncomfortable. She wasn't certain if *her* presence gave way to the most whispers, or if William's did; either way, when she whispered, "Perhaps we strangers should stick together," he even managed to smile.

With Jack and Jill behind him, Ethan disappeared into a room. The five guards dispersed, no doubt to gather everyone for the family meeting.

Elizabeth said something to Aunt Dolly, then walked off down the hall, leaving Celeste and William alone with the old woman, who considered them for a moment, then motioned for them both to follow her.

"It would be best to give Ethan some time alone right now," she said. "We'll convene in an hour or two; right now, however, there's not much to do but wait. I could show you around if you'd like; this house is a maze, and not likely to get any easier to navigate." She paused. "William, I'll give you a choice. You could go with Ethan or stay with me and Celeste. I doubt he'll need three of you for protection here, however."

"I'll go with you," William said after a moment's hesitation. "I don't-- remember much of the house. I'll need to know, if I am to stay."

"Do you *want* to stay?" Aunt Dolly asked.

"I would like to stay," William said, but he looked uncertain now, as if he wasn't sure how his presence would be received.

"Good." Aunt Dolly didn't seem to be surprised by this; nor was she upset. And Celeste realized how difficult it would be for him if he were to leave--if any of them wanted to leave, vampires, humans, or werewolves.

Being a member of a Household had its advantages, Celeste saw as they made their way through the house. Those who worked outside supported the family, but they weren't expected to pay for everyone's needs just from their income. The household grew most of its own food for the human members, bottled its own blood (from the human members; Aunt Dolly didn't say what the humans thought of that, but she did mention that no one was forced to donate.) There were other family-owned houses and businesses in the area that ensured no one in the family would ever want for anything, as long as the Hunters stayed on the other side of the wards.

And the Hunters were a large piece of the protections, of course. The front of the family as an odd religious cult was the brainchild of Aunt Dolly's father; according to the pictures hung on the hallway walls, the family had once dressed very differently than the modern clothing they wore now.

The disadvantages were not small in their own right. If someone were to leave in good standing, they were given a token amount of money to live on-- enough to live on for a little while--but they were not supported by the family beyond then. With the Hunters an ever-present threat, for vampires, striking out on your own wasn't exactly something one would call normal. Or safe.

And vampires liked to be safe.

The tension in the house was almost palpable. Aunt Dolly had to reassure no less than ten people who pulled her away with tears in their eyes. No one seemed to protest the family meeting, however; and no one mentioned Celeste or William's presence, save for a few of the children, who stared at Celeste with wide eyes before their parents whisked them away.

They circled around a room that seemed to be full of activity, and Celeste found out why when they reached that room. It was the meeting room, and also a dining room big enough for at least fifty people; the kitchen was right off the dining room, and someone had set out coffee and tea. There weren't many takers, however. The majority of the family ignored the chairs and opted to stand as well, grouped against the walls, as if for comfort. They fell silent when Aunt Dolly appeared with Celeste and William.

There was a table in the front of the room, set with six chairs.

"We'll be there," Aunt Dolly said. "Do you want something to eat or drink?" She lowered her voice. "I'll warn you--Vincent might be offended if you don't try the coffee. He blends it himself."

"Then I'll have a cup," Celeste said. She supposed she should feel uneasy, but the only vibes she felt from the people around her were grief and sadness, and fear of what was to come.

She followed Aunt Dolly to the table with her cup, and William took station behind her chair. Celeste wasn't sure how she should feel about having acquired a self-appointed bodyguard, but perhaps that was how he had managed to keep his panic at bay. No one seemed to have recognized him, at least, and after a moment, Celeste realized that they assumed he'd come with her.

Ten minutes after she sat down, a door opened behind her, and Ethan appeared with Jack and Jill at his back. For a moment, the silence in the room was absolute.

"Please," Ethan said. "Sit down." He'd changed his clothes and taken a shower, but even though he showed no sign of pain, he held himself stiffly, as if his wounds had not quite completely healed.

He carried his bloody clothes, now folded, and he set them on the table for everyone to see.

Elizabeth appeared to sit beside him, and Aunt Dolly sat beside her. Celeste had somehow ended up beside Ethan, but when she went to move, he said, softly, "Please stay," so she did. And then, louder, he said, "Early this morning, my parents were murdered by Hunters. I'm sure you know the details now, so I won't recount them. But they were betrayed, and they died. And I would have died as well, if our neighbor--and new ally--Celeste had not found me." He indicated the clothing. "I was shot six times. If the Hunters had used silver bullets, I would not be here now. If my sister Elizabeth had gone with my parents as they'd planned, she wouldn't be here either. And that's not all."

He spoke--quietly, but with enough force that they all paid attention. "We have traitors in our midst. Most of them have been taken into custody by now. Two will be sentenced--here--in a few minutes."

"Sentenced by whom?" an older vampire asked. It could have been an innocent question; after all, Ethan had not declared himself the Head of Household. But somehow, Celeste doubted that.

"By me," Ethan said. "I do not intend to give up my birthright. If anyone has a problem with me or my decision, or if you wish to leave, feel free to do so. I will hold no one here unwillingly. But if your loyalty remains true to the family, then I will do my best not to betray it."

Celeste half-expected the older vampire to leave, but he merely nodded and sat down.

"Those who betrayed us also murdered one of our own and attempted the murder of two others," Ethan continued. "The family of those killed have been excused from this meeting."

A young girl about Erin's age started to cry. A woman who looked like her mother, perhaps, consoled her, murmuring into her ear as she held her close.

"One of my cousins involved herself in this as well," Ethan said quietly. "She wrote me a letter before she killed herself this morning. I'd like to read it to all of you, so everyone knows what nearly happened." He took out the envelope, opened it, and removed one piece of paper.

"Ethan,
By the time you read this, I will be dead. I can only hope you are not.
I have greviously betrayed both my loved ones and the family itself. Since I already know my sentence, I will carry it out myself.

Six months ago, I received a message that the Hunters were gathering to attack. We'd existed so long without issue, that I did not believe the message, at first. But I researched, and finally decided that the threat was real.

Before I could warn your parents, I was approached by members of the family, who had been compromised by the Hunters. Their names are: Anita and Jared Cummings, both human. They convinced me that if I did not remain silent, the Hunters would attack and slaughter the entire family. They had maps and sketches of nearly every family-owned property in town. They had a list of names. They even had my source. In short, they had everything.

The Hunters wished to throw us into chaos. Anita informed me that their plan would be unchallenged, because if I tried to warn anyone, they would immediately deliver the names and all the papers to the Hunters. She and her son kept close watch over my actions. She said the Hunters were poised to attack, and all they needed was the information. They are the reason why I have become such a hermit of late.

Their plan was to murder your parents and sister, and then execute you as well. If their plan had worked, the House would be without a leader, in disarray, and ripe for the taking.

There is a human girl, Erin, who saw too much. They intended to murder her as well, but I think I might have protected her well enough.

I ensured your sister would not be in the car with your parents. That was all I could do. I can only hope that you were able to find my note before they delivered the papers to the Hunters."

At that, Ethan lifted a briefcase and set it on the table. "Just in case you are wondering, these are the papers in question. Found in Anita Cummings' possession." He picked up Birdie's note again. "She writes, *I apologize for my actions, and hope my meager efforts are not in vain.* That's all."

"We're doomed, then," someone said, but Celeste couldn't see who it was in the crowd.

"No," Ethan said. "Not doomed. Not if what I intend to do works."

"And what do you intend to do?" the same older vampire asked.

"The Hunters wish to kill vampires," Ethan said. "And we have two traitors. I intend to give them what they want."

There were gasps, and cries, at this statement, as if Ethan had informed them that he intended to open the doors wide for the Hunters to enter. But then the older vampire smiled approvingly.

"I expect you'll need volunteers, then," he said.

"Yes, I will," Ethan said. "Two volunteers." He looked at the older vampire steadily. "Are you volunteering, Abel?"

"I am," Abel said.

The vampires caught on first, of course. The humans took a little while to realize what Ethan meant to do, but when they did, they seemed largely approving. Ethan had no trouble finding another volunteer.

Almost immediately afterwards, on some signal Celeste did not catch, two of the four guards brought in a woman and a young man, blindfolded, gagged, and bound, and sat them on two chairs right in front of Ethan's table. Celeste glanced back at William; he'd attempted to unobtrusively slide down the wall to the floor; Jack and Jill stood near him, impassive. When the guards removed the blindfolds, the woman's eyes widened; the young man, presumably her son, sat stoically, not even attempting to hide the fury in his gaze.

"Take the gags off," Ethan said, and the guards moved to obey.

"Spells?" Celeste asked, sotto-voice.

"The ropes are enchanted against magic," Ethan said, unconcerned. But despite his words, Anita had to make an attempt. She spat a spell, or curse or something, but both the guards and Ethan had expected an attempt, and the ropes held.

"Do you have anything to say for yourselves?" he asked. "I have Jared on conspiracy, treachery, attempted murder, and murder. Anita, your crimes are no less severe. Not only did you betray us--your family--you also kept prisoner what I believe to be a wrongly accused werewolf."

Murmurs rose among the gathered family. No one had mentioned a name, but in truth, there was only one werewolf story in this family, and only one name, which rose on everyone lips in furious whispers.

Anita had paled. She glanced around, obviously searching for any sign of William. "You would--welcome a murderer into your household?"

"I'm not so sure he was the murderer," Ethan said. "Do either of you wish to tell me what truly happened twelve years ago?"

"He was dead!" Jared blurted out. "I made sure of it!"

The murmurs and whispers rose into a roar. Ethan waited until the noise had died down before he said, "I need to know what happened, Jared."

"It won't save me," Jared said. "I'll take that knowledge to my grave."

From behind Celeste, still sitting on the floor, William spoke. "Then you know? You do know?"

Silence fell across the room in a wave. Neither Jared nor his mother spoke, but Celeste could read the guilt in their gazes; guilt and fear and fury.

Jack helped William stand back up. He stood with his back to the wall, slightly hunched, defensive; staring out at the family who had abandoned him.

Abel walked up behind Jared. The guards did not stop him, but he paused before touching the prisoner, waiting for Ethan's nod. And Ethan *did* nod.

"You do realize I'll know everything once I'm done with you?" Abel asked, almost conversationally. Jared hadn't heard him approach. He jerked in surprise, and tried to turn around to see who had spoken. Abel wrapped one hand around his neck, immobilizing him. "I will know *everything*. And I will make you speak."

Jared stared at William. Fear fought with the fury for what seemed like a long time, but he did not speak. He transferred his gaze to Ethan, then, and somehow managed to smile. "I will not speak."

"Then Abel can take you," Ethan said. "And just by your actions and the actions of your mother, I'll declare William absolved. Innocent. And I will blame you for that crime as well." He smiled. "See, Jared, it doesn't matter if you confess. I already know the truth. Abel will just confirm it."

Abel wrenched Jared's head sideways and lowered his mouth to the vein in his neck. Anita watched, horrified, as Abel drank Jared's blood, and then she whispered to William, "You were dead."

"Werewolves are harder to kill than you'd think," Jack said sharply, coming to William's defense.

Only after Abel then bit his wrist and pressed it against Jared's mouth did Anita realize what Ethan intended to do. Jared tried not to swallow; he tried to struggle, but human strength was no match for vampire strength. And when the other volunteer stepped up behind Anita, she didn't even struggle.

It was necessary, Celeste thought, not to hide this away. To bring it out into clear light, in front of everyone; so that no one could claim foul once the deed was done. And no one protested; some averted their gazes, others watched, plainly fascinated. Celeste had no idea what the rules were about turning humans into vampires, but she suspected Ethan would have to give permission. That he'd decided on this punishment--and no one had protested--spoke volumes. They'd accepted him, for better or for worse.

In truth, turning someone into a vampire was far too intimate of a process for Celeste's taste. So she watched the others as they watched Abel and Christopher turn the two prisoners.

When they were finished, and both Anita and Jared were slumped in their bonds, Abel said to Jared, "Tell them what you did."

And Jared struggled, but began to speak. She'd insulted him; an innocent child. And he'd followed her and her brothers and William, and watched as William and Ginger went to find shelter, and he'd brought a kitchen knife from the household's vast kitchen. And perhaps the thought of killing a child hadn't crossed his mind until he'd overpowered a werewolf, and dragged his unconscious form further into the barn, and then hit the little girl--even though she was a vampire, she was still a little girl--and she'd fallen, so he'd hit her again, this time with the knife--

Perhaps he hadn't intended her death from the beginning. But he had killed her.

William collapsed, then; his legs buckled and he would have fallen if Jack hadn't caught him. There was an empty seat next to Celeste, however, and with a questioning glance at Ethan (and a nod from Ethan, who didn't look surprised at all), she pulled out the chair and helped William onto it.

And now, from the crowd, there were murmurs of sympathy and quite a few tears.

Once Jared finished speaking, Ethan asked for volunteers to deliver the two prisoners to the Hunters. He had to choose between a dozen hands.

Fifteen minutes later, the prisoners were gone. Ethan remained, but he'd sent two of the guards with the volunteers, with an order to be back before dawn or they'd be given up for dead.

Even though they only intended to dump the prisoners on the Hunters' doorstep, something could very well go wrong.

After that, there were questions. And comments. And petitions. And more tears. But by midnight, the crowd had largely wandered off, leaving Ethan alone with Aunt Dolly, Celeste, the werewolves, Abel, and Aurora. Even Elizabeth had gone to sit with Erin.

By midnight, Abel had begun to usher the remnants of the crowd away. Ethan didn't protest; he looked tired, Celeste thought, which was not a surprise at all. Once they were all gone, Abel said, "Six bullets less than a day ago, and you look like hell, Ethan. I don't mean to intrude, but you need to rest."

"I know," Ethan said. "Thank you for sending them away."

"Most of what they wanted could have waited another day or two," Abel said.

"Normalcy is best," Ethan replied, and for a moment they stared at each other until Abel looked away.

Abel looked away.

"If that was the wrong decision, I'll find out soon," Ethan said when he didn't reply.

"No, it was the right decision," Abel said. "Normalcy is always best, especially when it involves the family. I'm sorry, Ethan. I liked your parents. We might not have seen eye to eye at times, but they were good people."

Ethan nodded, his eyes suddenly bright. He didn't speak; he didn't need to.

"It's past time we head to bed," Aunt Dolly said. She hadn't spoken much throughout the family meeting, just lent her presence to Ethan, a silent rock beside him. But now she put one hand on his arm. "Someone will wake you when they return, or if something were to go wrong. But Abel's right; you need to rest."

"I know," Ethan said, and looked around the room for a moment, as if to make sure everyone was gone. His gaze fell on Celeste. "Someone will take you home, I'm sure--"

"That's fine," Celeste said. "Or I can walk. I'm not exactly Hunter fodder."

"And we'll see you again soon?" Aunt Dolly asked.

"I think I need to speak with someone named Rebecca who wants weaving lessons," Celeste said. "And of course I'd be happy to welcome any of you into my home."

"As you are welcome here," Ethan said. "Thank you--" His eyes were still suspiciously bright.

"You're welcome," Celeste said. And then, gently, "Go to sleep, Ethan."

Through some great effort, the tears did not spill; he kept them from falling, but not without cost. He stood up, then, and nodded to Abel and Aurora, then turned to go. Jack and Jill fell into step behind him.

William stayed behind. "I'll see you home," he said before anyone could ask.

"We'll have to find you a place to sleep," Aunt Dolly said to William. "I'll see what I can do by the time you return."

William nodded.

No one challenged them or questioned them on their way out; Celeste let out a breath as soon as she stepped onto the front porch. At William's questioning glance, she said, "That wasn't quite what I expected."

"What did you expect?" William asked.

"More of an argument, I guess," Celeste said. "That's how it is in Faerie; I thought it would be the same here. But they're also grieving. When the shock wears off, will Ethan have trouble keeping his seat?"

"I hope not," William said. "I don't think so. A Walker has always been Head of Household, as far as I know. As long as the Hunters stay away--"

"They're rather persistent, aren't they?" Celeste asked. She'd never had any reason to seek out a Hunter, or speak to one, and she doubted they would listen to her. As far as she'd ever heard, they tended to be fanatical in their belief that vampires were evil. They would probably be ecstatically happy if the Veil was closed as well, but she'd always found it interesting that they still used magic, despite its 'difference' from the humans they claimed to have saved.

The driveway out of the Walker compound was more than a mile long. Celeste noticed another house--a single light shone through the trees--about halfway to the road, but no one challenged them as they passed by that driveway, and the house itself was a dark blot in the midst of the trees. The forest itself was silent and peaceful and quiet.

There were wards around the property, of course, and interior wards as well, all separate from each other just in case one fell. Like a ring of invisible fences around the main house, keeping the occupants safe. If the first ring of wards failed, the Hunters would have to get through the second ring, then the third, and even a fourth before they would reach the house. And the wards around the house were harder still.

She realized, then, that the vampires were very nearly prisoners behind their wards. They couldn't move around in public with the Hunters in the area--not if they wanted to live--and they were, essentially, trapped. Would Ethan be allowed to leave the house until the Hunter threat had passed? What if it never passed? Vampires lived for a very long time, barring accidents or Hunters. And Ethan was, after all, only fifteen years old.

How did the ones without families manage?

"Your thoughts are bleak," William said. "I can almost smell them."

"Not so bleak," Celeste said after a moment. "But not very happy, no. I think I'm trying to understand something that seems both familiar and alien to me. Familiar, because I grew up in Court, wanting nothing and surrounded by family. Alien, because we didn't have the threat of Hunters constantly hanging over our heads. How do you thrive in that sort of environment? How do you *survive?*"

They were almost to the cottage now, meeting no one, and nothing had looked so welcoming and yet so lonely at the same time.

"Sometimes you just have to pretend the threat doesn't exist," Ethan said from where he sat in the shadows on the front porch. "Or go crazy with the unfairness of it all."

He wasn't alone--both Jack and Jill stood on either side of him.

"If your aunt finds out you came here--" Celeste began.

"She'll do what?" Ethan asked. "Absolutely nothing."

"She'll yell," Celeste said, and walked up onto the porch. "With good reason. What if there were Hunters here, waiting for me to return?"

"There's no one here," Ethan said. "And I left my cell phone behind, anyway." He held it up to show her. "You didn't lock the door behind you."

"The wards are better than any lock," Celeste said.

"And we didn't want William to walk home by himself," Jack added.

William looked surprised--and a little pleased--at that.

"You either live your entire life in fear, or you learn to take risks, knowing that each time you take a risk, it could be your last," Ethan said softly. "I choose not to live in fear."

"That's a good choice," Celeste said. "And you are, of course, welcome here at any time. But right now--"

"It's time for us to go," Ethan said, and stood. He showed none of the weariness he'd shown only minutes before; Celeste had to wonder if that had been for show. "William? You can share a room with Jack and Jill for the time being if you'd like; we'll work on separate lodgings as soon as the dust settles from all of this."

"Your aunt seems to think you don't need three werewolves to keep you safe," William pointed out.

"I'm inclined to disagree," Ethan said. "At least for now."

William smiled. "Thank you."

They left her then, standing alone on the porch, disappearing into the forest as if they were ghosts. Three werewolves and a vampire. Nefir would have been proud. And envious.

Thinking of Nefir made her think of her family, and everything she'd left behind. She'd refused contact for almost a decade, and then sporadically since then. She hadn't actually seen her cousin in almost fifteen years.

She wanted to see him now.

Before she could talk herself out of it, she walked into the house, opened the storage chest, and took out a mirror wrapped in silk. She set it on the table beside the couch, sat next to it, and spoke the word to activate it. With bigger mirrors, you could set them up as portals, but this one was too small. Even so, if she ever decided to move back to Faerie, she could return in the space of hours, not days or weeks--with everything she wanted to take with her, as long as it fit through the mirror she intended to use.

It took the mirror a moment to connect. And when it did; when he cousin's slightly older face appeared, he looked genuinely surprised.

"Celeste?"

She sensed both wariness and concern in his voice. "Nefir. This is going to be awkward, I realize."

"Well, it's been a few years since I've seen your face," Nefir said. "I kept my promise. I stopped spying on you."

"I know you did," Celeste said. "And that's not why I'm calling. Are you free?"

Nefir smiled. "A king is never free," he said, which was true. "But I could carve out some time for my favorite cousin." Almost immediately, she saw that he regretted those words; he'd always been flippant, and she had never been his favorite cousin. But tonight was not the night to take offense.

"Could you come here if I open a portal in the other mirror?" Celeste asked. She nearly asked 'would', but that would imply that it was his choice, not hers. And she wanted this to be her choice alone.

"Of course," Nefir said, curious now. "But may I ask the occasion for this meeting? Did something happen? Are you okay?"

"Something happened that made me realize the importance of family," Celeste said. "I'm fine. And I'm still not coming back quite yet." He would notice that she'd said 'not quite yet', which was a marked difference from her previous words of 'not in this century'. "I'll tell you about it when you come."

"Very well," Nefir said. "Open the mirror, and I will come. Do you need anything? Can I bring you food? Or drink? Your favorite wine?"

"A bottle of wine," Celeste said, because of course he would remember her favorite wine. "It's not a celebration, however. More of a wake."

"A wake," Nefir said, almost cautiously. "Someone close to you died?"

"Someone I never met died," Celeste said. "And I saved their son's life."

"I see," Nefir said. "And you intend to tell me what happened?"

"If you'll listen," Celeste said. "Give me five minutes. I'll activate the mirror." She walked into the living room and uncovered a large, ornate mirror that sat against the wall. The words to activate the spell came easily to her lips, but still she hesitated before speaking them, not sure she wanted Nefir in her home just yet.

But it was too late now.

He carried a small bottle in his hand, but nothing else. Homemade wine. Potent stuff. Celeste hadn't tasted it since she'd left Faerie. The humans had no equivalent; theirs tasted more akin to water.

When he caught sight of her face, he paused, one hand on the mirror, poised to go back to Faerie and leave her in peace. "I'm not certain you truly want me here," he said. "I could leave the bottle--"

"No," Celeste said, and favored him with a small smile. "Come. Sit with me out on the porch. I'll tell you what happened. It involves vampires."

Nefir brightened up, just as she expected he would. "Vampires? Where are we, exactly?"

"Somewhere in Kentucky, and that's all you'll know for now," Celeste said seriously. "And you're not to bother them."

"Very well," Nefir said, and settled into a chair. The darkness was more soothing than cloying, at least; she could pretend his presence did not matter quite as much as it did. He opened the bottle, and poured them both a glass. The smell of it drifted towards her, reminding her of home.

And as she drank, she told him what had happened and what she had done. And when she was finished, he told her news from Faerie--from *home*-- and with the wine clouding both judgment and memory, they talked long into the night and near to dawn.

Nefir did not ask her to return to Faerie--not once. He did not cajole her, or question her; he merely listened and responded in turn. This was unlike the Nefir she knew before; the grieving one; the one who had almost banished her from the kingdom for daring to defy him.

Perhaps time *did* heal wounds, after all. And perhaps one day she'd return home. Somehow, the possibility did not seem so impossible now.

Not at all.

If you enjoyed this author's book, then please place a review up at the site of purchase and any social media sites you frequent!

You can find ALL our books up on our website at:
http://www.writers-exchange.com

All Jennifer's books:
http://www.writers-exchange.com/Jennifer-St-Clair/

all our fantasy novels:
http://www.writers-exchange.com/category/genres/fantasy/

About the Author

Jennifer St. Clair grew up in Southern Ohio and spent most of her childhood in the woods around her home. She wrote her first novel when she was thirteen, and hasn't stopped since. She lives with her ball python, Fester, and two cats, Ash and Rowan.

In her spare time, she crochets, makes cloth dolls, collects antiques, books, and vintage clothing, and takes digital photographs with varying degrees of success.

Her *Beth-Hill series* is set in the area in America that contains many supernatural creatures: Wild Hunt, Vampires, Dragons, Faery and more.

It is part of the Universe that her *Jacob Lane Series, Karen Montgomery Series* and vampire trilogy, *The Shadow Series* are set in.

Follow all her books on her author page:

http://www.writers-exchange.com/Jennifer-St-Clair/

If you want to read more about other books by this author, they are listed on the following pages...

A Beth-Hill Novel (Stand Alone Novels)

Are creatures of the night and all manner of extramundane beings drawn to certain locations in the natural world? In the Midwestern village of Beth-Hill located in southern Ohio, the population is made up of its fair share of common citizens...and much more than its share of supernatural residents. Take a walk on the wild side in this unusual place where imagination meets reality.

Blood of Innocents

Ten years ago, Orien, crown prince of the Seleighe, was captured by his mortal enemies, locked in a dungeon and turned into a vampire. Six years into Orien's sentence, the Healer's brother Cullen disobeyed his mistress's orders to kill him and turned him into a vampire instead, thus sealing both their fates for all eternity.

Now both Orien and Cullen are set free. But a secret only Cullen knows lies locked inside his mind, threatening to drive him mad before he can uncover the identity of a traitor--the very elf who betrayed Orien and left them both to die in darkness.

Publisher: http://www.writers-exchange.com/blood-of-innocents/

Full Moon

Werewolves change into wolves when the moon is full. But Edward's curse only allows him to be *human* when the moon is full.

Alone and despairing, Edward hides himself away from the world. He's scraped out a meager existence for himself for almost a century in the forest he's grown to love and call home. But in the depths of a terrible winter, he stumbles across clues from the life his mother left behind in Faerie. The truth may give him the answers he needs about the source of his birthright... and the curse that holds him captive.

Publisher: http://www.writers-exchange.com/full-moon/

A Beth-Hill Novel: Jacob Lane Series

Are creatures of the night and all manner of extramundane beings drawn to certain locations in the natural world? In the Midwestern village of Beth-Hill located in southern Ohio, the population is made up of its fair share of common citizens...and much more than its share of supernatural residents.

Jacob Lane is a ten-year-old girl who's spent her life unaware of her magical heritage. After being sent to Darkbrook, a school of magic, supernatural mysteries seem to spring to life all around her and her new friends.

Book 1: The Tenth Ghost

After Jacob Lane's parents mysteriously vanish, she's sent to Darkbrook, the only school of magic in the United States. While there, she and her new friends stumble upon a series of mysterious deaths in the nine ghosts that haunt the halls of Darkbrook. These ghosts were students who died at the school over the past hundred years. Will Jacob become the tenth ghost, or can she stop a witch's reign of terror?

Publisher: http://www.writers-exchange.com/the-tenth-ghost/

Book 2: The Ninth Guest

When Jacob's friend Ophelia's family decides to open up their castle for guests, amateur paranormal sleuth Jacob Lane is invited to join in on the fun. "Spend the night in a vampire's castle and live to tell the tale!" is supposed to be a fundraiser to help Ophelia's family pay the bills. Heating a castle costs quite a bit, after all. But, after the truth of an old secret is uncovered, what began as an innocent business venture soon turns deadly when vampire hunters get involved.

For years, the vampire hunters have had only one goal: To destroy all vampires. With the help of a new friend, Jacob and Ophelia must work together to save the entire VonBriggle family from extinction.

Publisher: http://www.writers-exchange.com/the-ninth-guest/

Book 3: The Eighth Room

For two hundred years, the Selkies have kept themselves separate from those who live on land. But now the Selkies need allies or they'll be crushed by their ancient enemies, the Finfolk.

Jacob and Ophelia, students at the only school of magic in the United States, uncover a mystery that dates back to Darkbrook's beginnings. While helping clean out old storage rooms for classroom expansion, they find something that might save the Selkies from extinction. With the help of the youngest member of the Wild Hunt who are no longer so wild or terrifying, they must foil the Finfolk who desire the Selkie's destruction...or die trying.

Publisher: http://www.writers-exchange.com/the-eighth-room/

Book 4: The Seventh Secret

After a picture of Niklas, the dragons' liaison to the only school of magic in the United States, shows up in too many newspapers to count, Darkbrook is forced to go on the defensive. The secret of Darkbrook's existence has been discovered. But there are more than dragonhunters in the forest, and, as Jacob Lane, supernatural sleuth and student at Darkbrook, learns how to use her newly discovered talent of healing, she helps to right an old wrong and must battle a teenaged wizard intent on proving--once and for all--that magic is real.

Publisher: http://www.writers-exchange.com/the-seventh-secret/

Book 5: The Sixth Stone

Jacob Lane, supernatural sleuth, and Danny, her werewolf friend, stumble across an alternate world where the Wild Hunt was never bound, and Darkbrook, the school of magic they attend, was abandoned a hundred years ago.

But when the Hounds of the Hunt wish to surrender, the two students are swept up in a whirlwind of heartbreak, betrayal, and the discovery of a lost treasure.

Publisher: http://www.writers-exchange.com/the-sixth-stone/

A Beth-Hill Novella: Karen Montgomery Series

Are creatures of the night and all manner of extramundane beings drawn to certain locations in the natural world? In the Midwestern village of Beth-Hill located in southern Ohio, the population is made up of its fair share of common citizens...and much more than its share of supernatural residents. Take a walk on the wild side in this unusual place where imagination meets reality.

Karen Montgomery was an ordinary woman until she stumbled into the extraordinary... A bargain with elves worth its weight in gold. A plague of sinister ladybugs. Rogue vampire hunters, including one who tries to turn over a new leaf--with disastrous consequences. A ghostly huntsmen of the Wild Hunt wishing for redemption. Karen's life will never be the same again.

Book 1: Budget Cuts

Karen Montgomery is used to taking care of the unpleasant jobs no one else wants to deal with. When a shortage of funds forces her to fire fifteen employees from the library, she isn't happy, but the nasty task has to be done and she is, after all, the boss. But Karen finds finishing her task impossible when she can't seem to track down Ivy Bedinghaus, a night clerk she's never actually met. Once she finally does confront Ivy, she's thrust into a centuries-old conflict that makes her previous troubles radically pale in comparison.

Publisher: http://www.writers-exchange.com/budget-cuts/

Book 2: The Secret of Redemption

Karen Montgomery, librarian, finds herself embroiled in another otherworldly adventure...

A member of the Wild Hunt--ghostly myths that aren't so ghostly (or myth-like) anymore--needs help in reconciling who he once was in life and who he is now.

A little girl has gone missing. And the one most likely responsible for her disappearance is the one Karen must prove innocent.

Publisher: http://www.writers-exchange.com/the-secret-of-redemption/

Book 3: Ladybug, Ladybug

An innocent attempt to rid the library of a plague of ladybugs turns sinister when a rogue vampire hunter gets the contract for pest control.

Ivy Bedinghaus, who works for Karen as a night clerk--along with all the vampires in Beth-Hill--are in danger, and their only hope for survival is with the help of Karen, a member of the Wild Hunt, and Russell Moore, a reformed vampire hunter.

Publisher: http://www.writers-exchange.com/ladybug-ladybug/

Book 4: Detour

One wrong turn sends Karen down a road that shouldn't exist, to the site of an old accident and an even older mystery. With reformed vampire hunter Russell Moore's help, Karen finds the key to the mystery. But Russ keeps his own secrets...some of which are deadly.

When old friends from Russ' past come to call, Karen realizes his secrets might just mean his doom. After a terrible incident three years ago, before Karen met him, Russ wants only to live the rest of his life quietly in Beth-Hill. But his secret might not allow him the new lease on life Russ longs for.

Publisher: http://www.writers-exchange.com/detour/

Companion Story: Russ' Story: Capture

Long before Russell Moore ever met supernatural sleuth Karen Montgomery or set foot in Beth-Hill, he was a vampire hunter, possibly the best vampire hunter of all. He brought down whole nests of vampires, caring little about the consequences of his actions. Anyone who lived with or helped the vampires became enemies to be slaughtered.

So what kind of an idiot would capture a ruthless vampire hunter without a conscience and try to reform him?

Ethan Walker was that idiot. Wanting to protect his family, Ethan set out to prove to Russ that vampires weren't all evil, soulless creatures. If Russ would allow himself to witness their lives, see their humanity, surely he and other vampire hunters like him would let them live in peace. *Surely?*

Publisher: http://www.writers-exchange.com/capture/

Secrets When in Shadow Lie

Twelve years ago, Ryan Grey was cursed by a witch to hide a secret. He's lived with the curse of being unable to die permanently, and, over the years he's slowly losing the memory of his past until almost nothing remains.

But now, after a chance meeting with an elf named Zipporah, he discovers the key to unlocking the secret and breaking the curse once and for all...if he can survive the breaking.

Publisher: http://www.writers-exchange.com/secrets-when-in-shadow-lie/

The Dead Who Do Not Sleep

Will Spark only wants a good night's sleep after a night of drinking. Instead, two thugs bang on his door, demanding answers to questions he can't understand. And then they killed him...

Publisher: http://www.writers-exchange.com/the-dead-who-do-not-sleep/

A Beth-Hill Novel: The Abby Duncan Series

Are creatures of the night and all manner of extramundane beings drawn to certain locations in the natural world? In the Midwestern village of Beth-Hill located in southern Ohio, the population is made up of its fair share of common citizens...and much more than its share of supernatural residents. Take a walk on the wild side in this unusual place where imagination meets reality.

Situated in Beth-Hill, where imagination meets reality, is The Rose Emporium, owned by elderly and not-a-little-odd Rose Duncan. The large Victorian house smackdab in the middle of nowhere is a cross between a pawn shop and an antique store that caters to supernatural creatures needing to barter. Rose's twenty-something niece, Abby Duncan, discovers that the world isn't made up of just run-of-the-mill, ordinary humans but an entire spectrum of unusual beings. With her preconceptions about what's normal and what's not turned upside-down, Abby is in for a whole lot of startling truths, mysteries-- about herself and the people and places around her--and danger.

Novella 1: By Any Other Name

Woodturner Abby Duncan decides to sell her spindles at a local Renaissance Festival with only some success. After all, no one really spins their own yarn anymore, do they? While there, she discovers that one of her newfound friends is not what he appears--and his secret is about to get him killed!

Publisher: http://www.writers-exchange.com/by-any-other-name/

Book 2: The Uncrowned Queen

Abby Duncan's elderly Aunt Rose has always been a bit odd. And now she's off on a mysterious trip, leaving Abby behind to run the Rose Emporium, an unusual sort of antique shop. Such an extraordinary store would have been a perfect place for Seth and the others, her friends from the Renaissance Festival, to take a break from traveling between Faires. But when tragedy strikes and Abby and the others discover the true nature of the Rose Emporium, they'll have to travel into Faerie itself before their tightknit group is whole again.

Abby doesn't know much about her family history, but she's about to find out the truth...whether she likes it or not.

Publisher: http://www.writers-exchange.com/the-uncrowned-queen/

Book 3: Hunter

Winston Matthew Delaney, a former vampire hunter, has been sentenced to seven years labor at Madame Mim's Teahouse. In his late thirties, Winston has spent most of his life strongly believing that vampires have no place in the world and his purpose was to eliminate them. He'd been training his own apprentice Josh to believe the same when he was captured. Josh continues to seek out his master and rescue him. But, shocking himself most of all, Winston discovers a truth that changes everything he's ever believed and based his principles on: Most vampires have no desire to kill and proliferate; instead, they only want to live their lives in peace.

Arabella Bauer believes her brother died in a car accident. In part, that's true. But he was a no-good drunk and actually caused the accident that took the life of one of the men in the other car involved. Only Colin survived. Despite being badly injured himself, Colin killed Arabella's brother in retaliation.

Arabella is contacted by Josh, who attempts to win her over into believing vampires are real. He gives her information that leads her to The Rose Emporium...and Colin, a vampire...

Publisher: http://www.writers-exchange.com/hunter/

A Beth-Hill Novel: The Shadows Trilogy

Are creatures of the night and all manner of extramundane beings drawn to certain locations in the natural world? In the Midwestern village of Beth-Hill located in southern Ohio, the population is made up of its fair share of common citizens...and much more than its share of supernatural residents. Take a walk on the wild side in this unusual place where imagination meets reality.

A Dreamer dreams the future when the past is not yet laid to rest. Ten years ago, a plague swept across the Seven Kingdoms. Ten years ago, the Queen of Iomar's son was exiled and named the author of the magical plague. Now, in the present, Terrin works to complete his ultimate goal: Control of the Seven Kingdoms using his son's power to supplement his own. But his attempt at dominion meets resistance and the fate of the world rests in the unlikely hands of an exiled prince, a Dreamer, and a vampire...

Book 1: The Prince of Shadows

When Alban's father Terrin appeared at the castle door with a vampire in tow and apologies on his lips, Alban fell under his spell just like everyone else and welcomed him home. But Terrin didn't return to live quietly in his brother's kingdom. He had other plans and, with Alban's untrained powers at his disposal, he begins his ruthless plan to destroy the Seven Kingdoms and rule them all, beginning with his brother's death.

Terrin engineers events to cast the blame on his nephew, Teluride, intending to see the boy executed for his father's murder. But there are those who would thwart Terrin in his mad plan for power, and Alban forms an unlikely alliance with Skade, the reclusive Queen of Iomar, and Terrin's slave, a young vampire with no memory of his name or origins. Although the future looks grim, Alban and the vampire attempt to stop Terrin...and they almost succeed.

A darker history lies at the heart of Terrin's treachery, and only Skade knows the true reason why Terrin would murder his own brother and attempt to destroy both Alban and the vampire to achieve his goals. The Ghost who resides in Skade's mirror--her servant and thrall--holds one of the keys to Terrin's madness. Unfortunately, more than one person wishes for the past to remain the past and the future to hold no shadows of what might have been...

Publisher: http://www.writers-exchange.com/the-prince-of-shadows/

Book 2: Lost In Shadows

Events set in motion ten years ago come to a head as Skade, the reclusive Queen of Iomar, and Nicodemus, who is imprisoned by Skade, struggle to free Alban and the vampire from Terrin's grasp. Old secrets come to light when Skade's exiled son is forced to face his past--or die trying to redeem himself once and for all. Can the crimes of the past truly be forgiven? Only time will tell...and time is running out.

Publisher: http://www.writers-exchange.com/lost-in-shadows/

Book 3: Bound In Shadows

With his power crushed, brother to the king and father to Alban, Terrin is forced to take drastic measures to regain his sons after they are freed and harness the power they possess. But he has an ally inside the healer's house where they are recovering who works to further his plans. The Queen of Iomar, Skade's son, courts redemption to try to save his mother's life, and the vampire who no longer remembers his own name dreams a dream that might save them all...or damn them if success is thwarted.

Publisher: http://www.writers-exchange.com/bound-in-shadows/

A Beth-Hill Novel: Wild Hunt Series

Are creatures of the night and all manner of extramundane beings drawn to certain locations in the natural world? In the Midwestern village of Beth-Hill located in southern Ohio, the population is made up of its fair share of common citizens...and much more than its share of supernatural residents. Take a walk on the wild side in this unusual place where imagination meets reality.

The Wild Hunt roamed the forest outside of Beth-Hill until the Council bound them for a hundred years. Nevertheless, a century of existence has made an indelible mark not easily forgotten for these ghostly myths that are no longer so ghostly or myth-like...

Book 1: Heart's Desire

The Wild Hunt roamed the forest outside of Beth-Hill until the Council bound them for a hundred years--a lifetime for a human but only a passing thought to one such as Gabriel, Master of the Wild Hunt. As the Council's binding draws to a close, old enemies reappear to ensure that the Wild Hunt is bound once more--to a creature much worse than the Council has been.

Publisher: http://www.writers-exchange.com/hearts-desire/

Book 2: Fire and Water

As a young vampire, Erialas Morgan brought his mother back to life with a spell that shouldn't exist, shouldn't have worked...perhaps shouldn't have been performed at all. Desperation and love are his only excuses for doing the unthinkable.

There are others who wish to use that same spell for their own gain--and to destroy the Wild Hunt once and for all. Caught in the middle of a war between the Morgan clan of vampires and their human kin, Erialas turns to the Hunt for help. But even Gabriel, the Master of the Wild Hunt, may not be able to stop the tide of death and destruction once it turns.

Publisher: http://www.writers-exchange.com/fire-and-water/

Book 3: The Lost

Almost sixty years ago, Darkbrook, the only school of magic in the United States, opened its doors to students of decidedly different natures, sending out letters of invitation to the elves, the dragons, and the vampires. The three who responded to the invitation banded together despite their differences but vanished only weeks later along with an entire classroom full of students and their teacher after a field trip gone horribly wrong.

The Wild Hunt has healed and the Hounds have grown closer together, keeping Darkbrook's forest safe and secure for those who live there. Malachi, one of the eldest members of the Wild Hunt, has adapted to Josiah's spell to help him see, but when a demon boy trapped in the body of a human body for sixty years inside the school disrupts the newfound calm, the Hunt--and those they protect--are thrust into a struggle that should have ended long ago when a vampire, an elf, and a dragon vanished into the Mists.

Publisher: http://www.writers-exchange.com/the-lost/

Book 4: A Glint of Silver

Jericho is a vampire who wants is to live away from the Richmond household of vampires led by his ruthless father Connor. When Jericho tries to escape, Connor punishes him and leaves him to die. Tristan is determined to be the one to bring Jericho back, but he can't see him suffer for wanting a normal life. As long as Connor lives, Jericho will never be safe or free. As long as Connor *lives*...

Publisher: http://www.writers-exchange.com/a-glint-of-silver/

Book 5: All That Glitters

As a member of the cruel Morgan Household of vampires, twelve-year-old Arthur Morgan has been abused all his life.

Maya, a water fairy, shows him just how horrible and twisted the household he's grown up is. With her help, and the unexpected help of an adult vampire, Arthur attempts to escape.

Can he become something more than what his father has decreed?

Publisher: http://www.writers-exchange.com/all-that-glitters/

Book 6: Family Matters

Weaver Celeste is an elf living in exile in the human world. She's renting a house near the Walker Household, made up of vampires with whom she hasn't yet been introduced. Early morning, right before dawn, she witnesses a Hunter attack that kills fifteen-year-old Ethan

Walker's human parents. Ethan, the vampire who leads the Walker Household, is the only survivor. Even as Celeste saves his life and gives him a place to hide while he recovers, a coup attempt is unfolding in the Walker Household. Can the vampires loyal to Ethan not only capture those involved but unearth proof that the same people were involved in covering up an old crime before the sun sets?

Publisher: http://www.writers-exchange.com/family-matters/

The Chelsea Chronicles

Normally a quiet, serene place, Chelsea Kingdom seems like the perfect location for a centuries' old vampire to blend in and live a normal life, even escape hunters and an angry mob. Unfortunately, his timing couldn't be worse...

Book 1: So You Want to be a Vampire

Chelsea Kingdom is usually a pretty quiet place but recent murders--committed by a vampire--upset the calm. Newcomer to town, Vlad Dhalgren wants only to blend in and live a normal life. He quickly learns that isn't possible, given that other vampires have been hiding in the shadows around the castle--in plain sight--for years.

Despite her lineage, Anna Everett, the crown princess of the Kingdom of Chelsea, isn't a wizard like her father, which means she will never be Queen. She has only one friend, Valerian Moreton--Val--who has secrets he's never shared that could get him *and* Anna killed...

Publisher: http://www.writers-exchange.com/so-you-want-to-be-a-vampire/

Book 2: Transformation

As Anna, crown princess of Chelsea, adjusts to life as a vampire after recent events, Vlad plans for a future he has no real hope to seeing come to pass due to injuries sustained while attempting to save Anna's life. But, as life goes on for Anna and her friend Valerian "Val" Moreton, it changes for others--some of whom are not quite what they seem...

Publisher: http://www.writers-exchange.com/transformation/

You can find ALL our books up on our website at:

http://www.writers-exchange.com

All Jennifer's books:

http://www.writers-exchange.com/Jennifer-St-Clair/

all our fantasy novels:

http://www.writers-exchange.com/category/genres/fantasy/

www.ingramcontent.com/pod-product-compliance
Lightning Source LLC
Chambersburg PA
CBHW061335120726

48001CB00002B/878